"This isn't r[...] "You can't go on this wa[...] o the play—"

Erin dug her nails into the blond girl's palm. "*Please*, don't say a word to Ms. Thornton, Shara, okay? Not one word."

"You know I won't. But I can't stand to see you hurting like this."

"I want that part, Shara. And I'm not going to let these stupid headaches stop me." She was dizzy now and very nauseous. She braced herself on the car while Shara fumbled with the key.

"Even if you have to play opposite David Devlin?" Shara asked shakily.

Erin tried to nod, but every movement sent fresh waves of agony shooting through her head. "Even that," she whispered, falling across the seat as the door opened.

TIME TO
LET GO

Lurlene McDaniel

BANTAM BOOKS
NEW YORK · TORONTO · SYDNEY · AUCKLAND

RL 5, age 10 and up

TIME TO LET GO

A Bantam Book / August 1995
Previous Bantam edition published January 1991

ISBN: 0-553-28350-2

Published simultaneously in the United States and Canada

PRINTED IN THE UNITED STATES OF AMERICA

OPM   16 15 14 13 12 11 10 9

I'd like to express my appreciation to Roses Colmore-Taylor, M.Ed. of REACH, Chattanooga, Tennessee.

"Blessed are they that mourn: for they shall be comforted."

—MATTHEW 5:4 (KJV)

TIME TO
LET GO

Chapter One

~⚬~

"By your silence I sense that you'd rather be anywhere but here talking with me. And I'm also assuming it wasn't your idea to come."

Erin Bennett glared at Dr. Roberta Richardson and released an exaggerated sigh. "There's nothing to talk about. I don't need a psychiatrist to pick my brain apart."

"I'm not a psychiatrist; I don't dispense medications in my practice. I'm a professional counselor, a family therapist, and your parents are concerned about you and thought I could help—"

"Help how? I'm perfectly fine. It's my parents who need counseling."

"Why do you say that?"

"Because they're the ones who're making me come here. There's nothing wrong with me. It's *them*."

Dr. Richardson pressed her fingertips together and leveled soft brown eyes at Erin sitting on the other side of the polished oak desk. Quietly she said, "'Perfectly fine' seventeen-year-old girls don't have incapacitating, unexplained headaches."

Erin winced, remembering the fierce pain that

came on with little warning. The doctors had referred to them as "migraines," even though they weren't altogether typical of most migraines. Erin didn't care what they called them. She only knew that they were interfering with her senior year at Briarwood. "I'm sure there's a good explanation," she said stubbornly.

Dr. Richardson opened the manila folder on her desk. "According to all the testing you've undergone in the past two months, there's no physiological reason for them. 'No reasonable medical explanation,'" Dr. Richardson read from the open file folder. "Looks as if they covered everything from brain tumors to epilepsy."

Erin shuddered, remembering how they'd injected dye into her veins and taken endless X-rays of her head while she lay perfectly still on a hard metal table. *Like a corpse,* she thought. *Or a person in a coma.* "They just haven't found the cause yet. Doctors don't *know* everything. Just because they can't figure it out is no reason to tell my parents that I'm some kind of a nut case."

"I know you're not a nut case, but aren't you concerned about your headaches?"

Erin felt her anger and resentment turning into tears, but she held them back. "Yes," she whispered, miserably, wanting to add, *"More than anything."* In the past month Erin had gotten sick twice at school and had to go home. Sometimes she had bad dreams in which her head was hurting, and when she awoke, she really did have a severe headache. "But I'm taking medicine for them," Erin told

Dr. Richardson. In the previous few months, Erin had been popping aspirin every day, and when her parents dragged her to a specialist, he gave her stronger pills that relieved the headaches but also wiped her out.

"Sometimes medications only relieve symptoms and never deal with the cause," Dr. Richardson continued. "Good health is more than treating bodily ailments. Human beings are made up of *soma*—body—and *psyche*—soul. I believe that you shouldn't treat one without treating the other."

"Are you saying that my headaches are all in my imagination?"

"Absolutely not. They're real enough. But it's important to look at the whole person, not just the malady, before seeking a cure." Dr. Richardson shoved the folder aside and said, "I'm glad you're here, Erin, and I'd like to get to know you better."

Erin felt like saying, "I don't want to know you better," but thought better of it. She didn't want her parents coming down on her the way they were always coming down on each other. Her mother was forever working at her boutique, and when she *was* at home, she was yelling about something or other at her husband.

Erin didn't think her father was doing so great either. He stayed away from the house, using his teacher's job at Briarwood as an excuse, but when he was home, he acted so withdrawn that he might as well be gone. Maybe if Amy were still around, things would be different.

It had been a hard summer after Amy's death, but with the new school year half-over, life was back to normal. If only her parents would stop their fighting. And if only she didn't have these blasted headaches—

"How's school going?" Dr. Richardson was asking.

"All right," Erin said, forcing herself to concentrate. The topic seemed safe enough, so she continued. "Ms. Thornton—she's the dance teacher at Briarwood—announced today that we're doing a joint play production with Berkshire Prep."

"The boy's school? When?"

"After Easter."

Dr. Richardson glanced at her desk calendar. "Only two months from now. Sounds like a big task. What's the play?"

"*West Side Story.*"

The willowy, brown-haired therapist smiled. "That was always one of my favorites. I saw the movie five times when it first came out in the sixties. Are you going for a part?"

Erin fidgeted with the buttons on her blouse. "I love to dance. I'd like the lead—Maria."

"You sound as if you may not try out. Why?"

The headaches, she thought, refusing to meet Dr. Richardson's eyes. "No reason. I guess I'll go for it. Auditions are next Monday, and the Berkshire drama department is supposed to come to our school for them."

"I guess it makes sense to do a joint production. It wouldn't be much fun playing a love scene with a girl dressed up like a guy, would it?" Dr. Richardson leaned across the desk and added, "I hope whoever gets the role of Tony is *gorgeous*."

Erin hadn't thought about the male lead until then. "It doesn't matter to me. Just so long as he's good."

"Do you have a boyfriend? Maybe he won't want you to play opposite some other guy. Would that be a problem?"

Erin felt herself tense up. The last boy she'd cared about had been Travis Sinclair. Dark-haired, brown-eyed, Berkshire Prep senior, Travis. Amy's Travis. The betrayer. "No. I'm too busy with dance and school. I don't have time for a boyfriend."

"Really? You're so pretty—"

Erin stood. "Look, I don't want to talk anymore today. I've got stuff to do, and I'll bet you have other people to see. People who really need a shrink."

Dr. Richardson rose and stepped forward. "Your hour's not up, Erin. You don't have to leave."

"This is a stupid idea, coming here to talk about my headaches. I feel fine, and I haven't had one in a week."

"Until we figure out what's causing them, they won't stay away. Won't you let me help you, Erin?"

The bright, airy office seemed suddenly small and confining. Erin wanted out. But she kept seeing the stern set of her mother's mouth as she'd told her, "You're going to see this counselor, and that's final. We've spent a fortune on medical tests, and everything's come back negative."

Erin had shouted, "Would you rather they'd found some horrible disease?"

"How could you suggest such a thing?" Her mother's eyes had filled with tears, and Erin wished she could have taken back the words. "We have to get to the bottom of this. I've already lost one daughter. . . ."

". . . week, same time?"

With a start Erin realized that Dr. Richardson was talking to her. "What?"

"Can you come back next week, same time?"

"I—uh—guess so. Sure."

Dr. Richardson smiled brightly. "Good. We can get rid of these headaches, Erin, if you trust me and let me help."

Erin didn't believe the therapist for a minute, but she'd go just so her parents would stop nagging her and shouting at each other. "Nobody has to know that I'm seeing a counselor, do they?" She dropped her gaze to the sea green carpet.

"Our discussions are in strict confidence, Erin. Only the people you choose to tell need ever know."

Fat chance! Erin told herself. She'd never let anyone find out. It was humiliating. "I still think the other doctors gave up too soon."

"Then prove it by working with me." Dr. Richardson's voice held a challenge.

Erin stared straight ahead as her mother's worried face floated in her mind's eye, along with the distant memory of her father crying over the decision to turn off Amy's life-support machines. "I guess I don't have any choice, do I?"

"See you next week."

Erin left without answering.

Chapter Two

"How did your meeting with Dr. Richardson go? What did you think of her?"

Erin shoved the food around on her dinner plate, figuring the best answer to her mother's question. "She was okay."

"Just okay? I liked her a lot when I met with her. I honestly think she can help you, Erin—"

Erin let go of her fork, and it clattered against her plate. "Look, this whole thing is your idea, you know. I never wanted to go see a counselor in the first place."

"It's for your own good. We only want to see you happy and well again."

"I'm *happy* going to school, dancing, planning for graduation and college, and doing things with my friends."

"Now don't go making too many plans. I'm not convinced that you need to go away to college. After all, the University of South Florida is a perfectly fine place, and it's right here in Tampa, so you could live at home—"

Here we go again, Erin thought. She interrupted her mother. "But USF doesn't have the dance department that Florida State does. I've told you that before."

"And if you're not well by September, you can't possibly consider moving away," her mother said stubbornly.

"I'll be okay, Mom."

"It's not a stigma to need help, Erin. There are lots of people—"

"Stop it," her father said curtly. "Erin, calm down. And Marian, get off Erin's back."

Mrs. Bennett glared at Mr. Bennett. "It was *your* idea too. We both agreed that she needed counseling."

"That's the point. It's *her* counseling. We agreed not to discuss her sessions, that she could talk about them only if she chooses."

"She's my daughter, my *only* daughter. I just want her to get well and lead a normal life again."

"It's her life, isn't it?"

They continued arguing, but Erin had stopped listening. She'd heard it all before over the past months, and no matter how it started, they always ended up in a yelling match, with Erin feeling like the catalyst. They argued about her, around her, because of her. Sometimes she heard them well into the night, and she had to cover her head with her pillow to shut them out.

It hadn't always been this way. They'd been happier together once, even as much as a year ago. Before Amy's accident.

"That's right," Mrs. Bennett was shouting. "Just walk right out in the middle of supper. That's the way to solve the problems—run away from them."

Mr. Bennett threw his napkin on the table and stood. "I've lost my appetite. I'm going to the library. I have papers to grade."

Mrs. Bennett followed him out of the dining room. "We certainly wouldn't want your family to get in the way of your job now, would we?"

"Me? What about you? You're always working late at that store of yours."

"I own my own business, and I have to manage it. I'm the boss, and the place would fall apart if I wasn't around."

"Well, since you're so indispensable, you won't miss me tonight."

"You've never turned down the money the store brings in, have you? And besides, it's going to take ten years to pay off our medical bills."

Erin squeezed her eyes shut, as if to block out the voices. What was happening to them? Why had her parents turned into strangers, and why was her family falling apart?

When Amy had been alive, their dinner table had been fun. She could still see Amy making them all laugh with her silly faces and involved stories about school. Sometimes, the way Amy hogged the limelight had irritated Erin, but now, looking back, she saw that Amy had definitely brought their family together. She'd acted as a kind of unifying force, compelling them to interact whether they wanted to or not! Erin suddenly realized that she'd give anything to have meals together again where they laughed and kidded instead of fought and argued.

She blinked away tears and began to clear the table, trying to ignore Amy's chair. It stood empty, yet ready and waiting, as if its former occupant might one day return.

Breathless, Erin slipped into the Briarwood theater back door and hurried to join the people sitting in a semicircle of metal chairs on the brightly lit stage. Her friend, Shara Perez, caught her eye and waved her over to the seat she'd been saving next to her. Ms. Thornton was talking to the group, and Mr. Ault, from the Berkshire drama department, stood beside her.

"Sorry I'm late," Erin whispered to Shara. "Did I miss anything?"

"Just the usual pep talk," Shara whispered back. "They'll start the auditions in a few minutes."

Erin heard Ms. Thornton saying, ". . . going to be a terrific production. Mr. Ault and I will be assigning major roles by Wednesday and passing out a rehearsal schedule on Friday. I expect every one of you to make every rehearsal. If you can't come to one, you must contact either me or Mr. Ault. Is that clear?"

Erin darted her eyes nervously, feeling as if Ms. Thornton was talking directly to her. Erin knew she had an excellent chance at the lead, but if she missed rehearsals because of the headaches, then Ms. Thornton might not choose her. Only the day before, during church, another one had come on her, and she'd spent the rest of Sunday in bed because of it.

Mr. Ault stepped forward. "Since this is a cold reading, we'll pass out the scripts now. Take a few minutes to look them over; then we'll have everybody break into smaller groups for the principal parts and let you read individually."

When she'd received her script, Erin asked Shara, "Are you going to read?"

"Don't have to," Shara told her. "Ms. Thornton already told me I'll be the singing voice of Maria. That way the lead only has to be responsible for her lines and the dancing. In fact, most of the parts will have stand-in singers. That way more people can participate."

"And those of us who can't carry a tune won't have to ruin the roles by attempting to sing," Erin observed. "That's pretty clever of Ms. Thornton."

Shara smiled. "I thought so, because those of us who can't dance won't have to worry about falling on our faces."

Pinky, a senior and a pixie-sized girl with black hair and a fiery Spanish personality, read for the part of Anita, the leader of the Puerto Rican girls. Erin's palms began to sweat because the reading for Maria was next, and by now she had her heart set on the part.

Erin read a scene, and when she was finished, Mr. Ault said, "I want you to try another one. But this time I want you to interact with the male lead."

He studied the group of boys who'd come forward for Tony.

Erin did too. One guy was particularly attractive, tall and lean with straight chestnut-colored hair and sexy smoke-colored eyes. She glanced at Shara, who gave a discreet thumbs-up gesture. All at once Erin realized that doing the play might be more fun than she'd originally thought.

Mr. Ault said, "David, come give this a try."

The dark-haired boy moved aside, and another one stepped forward, one not nearly so handsome. Erin judged him only about an inch or two taller than herself. His blond hair was tousled, a bit too long, hanging over his eyebrows in front and brushing his collar in the back. His eyes were bright blue, and they sparkled with mischief. He was wearing baggy checkered Bermuda shorts and a flamboyant floral-print shirt, socks that sagged and torn tennis shoes. Erin stared. Surely Mr. Ault was joking!

"Hi. I'm David Devlin," he said as he stood in front of her, offering a grin that lit up his face. "Did anyone ever tell you that you're the most beautiful girl this side of paradise city?"

Erin felt her mouth drop open and color creep up her neck.

"Uh—Erin? Do you want to get on with the reading, please?" Ms. Thornton's voice penetrated her trance. Totally flustered, Erin fumbled with the pages and dropped the script. The onlookers shuffled. David stooped, retrieved her booklet, and handed it back with another disarming smile. Erin took an instant dislike to David Devlin.

She snatched the booklet, found her place, and read the lines stiffly. David's expression grew serious as he fell into the character of Tony with amazing skill. At the end of the scene, Mr. Ault called, "Good job. You want to try it, Andy?"

Another boy came forward, and after he read, Mr. Ault sent in another one. Seth—Mr. Smoky Gray Eyes—read last with her. Other girls did the scene with each of the boys, and finally it was over.

"Okay, take a break," Ms. Thornton directed.

Shara hurried over to Erin. "You're a cinch," she said. "I saw Ms. Thornton and Mr. Ault taking notes the whole time."

Erin did several leg stretches and bend-overs to relieve the tension that had collected in her muscles. "Well, I certainly hope that they don't pick that David idiot to be the male lead," she said.

"Why not?" Shara said. "I think he's sort of cute. Not knock-you-out-cute, but adorable cute."

"So are three-year-olds, but I don't want to be in a play with one."

"As an objective bystander, allow me to tell you that he gave the best reading."

Erin rolled her eyes. "Just my luck." She took a chair to one side while activity buzzed around her and voices echoed in the cavernous theater. Beyond the lights the stage and seats were swallowed up by darkness. The wooden stage floor looked dusty, and the scrim curtain swayed slightly with a draft.

An unexplainable sense of loneliness descended on her. She stared at the others, feeling distant and removed. She loved the theater because she loved to dance, but she'd never wanted to be an actress. It had been her sister Amy who'd had greasepaint in her blood. Amy should be reading for a part. If only . . .

"I meant it when I said you're beautiful."

David Devlin's voice intruded into Erin's thoughts, and she looked up to see him standing beside her. "Just drop it," she told him sourly.

Instead he dragged a chair over and plopped down beside her. "So you're a dancer. I'm an actor. At least that's what I intend to be. Broadway and everything."

"Does that mean you can't dance?" she asked. "You can't take the male lead if you can't dance, you know."

"I can shuffle along," he said. " 'Course I'm not a pro, but I've taken classes before. Still, I'm a better actor than dancer, and I can sing. How about you?"

She ignored his question, saying, "You talk like you've already landed the part. You're not the only one trying out." To make her point Erin inclined her head toward Seth. She also hoped to convey to David that she found Seth a lot more appealing than she did him.

"He's decent," David said. "But I'm going to be playing Tony."

His attitude irritated her. "You'll excuse me if I cheer for the other guy."

David laughed. "You're pretty sure you're

going to get Maria, aren't you? What's the difference?"

"I—I am not sure at all," Erin stammered.

"Then why didn't you read for any other part?"

Disarmed by his logic, Erin was seething. "Well if you're a 'sure thing' for Tony, then I guess I should have read for another part." She stood, dropping her script.

David scooped it up. "You gotta learn to hang onto this thing, Erin."

Intent on brushing him off, Erin spun, only to have the back of her heel catch on the rung of the metal chair. It clanked and clattered and would have fallen if David hadn't reached out to steady it. "For a dancer you're a little clumsy," he teased. "Still gorgeous, however."

She couldn't think of a snappy put-down, and she considered throwing her script at him. Instead, she stalked off while he called, "See you on Friday, 'Maria.'"

Chapter Three

〜

"If he gets the part, I'll quit." Erin shoved dance gear into her duffel bag in the girl's locker room while Shara watched.

"Boy, I haven't seen you this worked up since Travis Sinclair took Cindy Pitzer to last year's Spring Fling dance."

"That was different," Erin snapped. "Amy was comatose, and that creep was dating someone else while he was supposed to be Amy's boyfriend. I hated him then, and I still do." She glared at Shara for making her remember. "I dislike David Devlin for entirely different reasons," she said.

Shara opened her locker and took out an apple. "Then you'd better consider quitting. According to the other guys at tryouts, he's the best. He wins every forensic competition and placed second in state in drama as a junior last year."

"What are you, a reporter?"

"I just asked a few questions, that's all. Besides, what better way to get to know Seth? Remember, the one with the sexy eyes?"

So Shara was interested in Seth. Erin hid her disappointment, saying, "No. They all seemed alike to me."

Shara buffed the apple on her shirt. "What's with you anyway, Erin? You're always snarling at people, and you're negative about everything. I was hoping that this play would be something fun we could do together."

"Nothing's wrong with me. I just happen to think David Devlin is a jerk, that's all."

"I don't think so," Shara countered. "Afterwards, after you stormed off, we were all getting acquainted and talking, and David had us in stitches imitating teachers at Berkshire. I laughed until I was crying, and I don't even *know* the teachers at Berkshire." Shara chuckled. "I can still picture him."

Exasperated, Erin slammed her locker door shut. "That sounds so juvenile. I wouldn't want to be a part of *ragging* on teachers. My father's a teacher here, remember?"

"Well, if we're all going to be in this play together, then you'd better join in. It's going to take all of us working like crazy to bring it off."

Erin realized Shara was right. She'd been in enough dance productions over the years to know how much hard work went into them. "We've got a couple of months, so there's plenty of time to get to know everybody." She zipped up her bag. A knot of tension had gathered at the base of her neck.

"The sooner, the better," Shara said. "I like the music, don't you?"

Erin was relieved that Shara had changed the subject and was forgetting their earlier disagreement. She didn't mean to argue with her friend. "Yeah, it's good music."

Shara broke into the words from the song "Tonight" and whirled around the locker room, her soprano voice echoing off the empty walls.

Erin listened to Shara's beautiful voice. It reminded her of springtime, and suddenly she imagined dandelion seeds floating above Amy's casket. A dull ache began to inch its way up her neck and lodge in the back of her head. "Be careful, or you'll fall down," she said to Shara.

Shara stopped twirling, then reached out and steadied herself on the bank of lockers. "Whoa! You're right. How do dancers twirl around and not get dizzy?"

The ache had spread to her forehead, and her eyes began to hurt. She rubbed them. "You have to focus on an object and every time you turn, you have to make sure you come back to that object."

"I guess that's why I sing," Shara said with a shrug. "Less danger of falling over."

Erin dropped to a bench. She began to see pinwheels of color, and the throbbing increased in her temples.

"Hey, you okay?" Shara asked. "You look white as a sheet."

"Did you drive your car today?"

"No, Dad dropped me off on his way to make hospital rounds. What's wrong, Erin? Another headache?"

Erin never tried to keep the headaches a secret

from her friend. Her parents had asked Dr. Perez for the names of specialists to treat her when the headaches had first started. "It came on real sudden."

"You want me to drive you home in your car?"

"Could you, please?"

Shara quickly gathered up their things. "Do you have your pills with you? Maybe you should take some."

"Yes, you're right." Pain stymied her. Why hadn't she thought of that? She found the pills, took two without water, and leaned against the lockers. Her breath was shallow. "I wish it didn't hurt so bad."

"Your doctors still haven't found what's causing them?"

"Not yet." By now Erin was feeling sick to her stomach. She gripped Shara's hand and allowed her friend to lead her out of the gym. Outside, the late-afternoon light stabbed at her eyeballs like hot needles.

"This isn't right, Erin," Shara muttered. "You can't go on this way. How are you ever going to do the play—"

Erin dug her nails into the blond girl's palm. "*Please*, don't say a word to Ms. Thornton, Shara, okay? Not one word."

"You know I won't. But I can't stand to see you hurting like this."

"I want that part, Shara. And I'm not going to let these stupid headaches stop me." She was dizzy now and very nauseous. She braced herself on the car while Shara fumbled with the key.

"Even if you have to play opposite David Devlin?" Shara asked shakily.

Erin tried to nod, but every movement sent fresh waves of agony shooting through her head. "Even that," she whispered, falling across the seat as the door opened.

"You need to think of your headaches as a *friend*, Erin," Dr. Richardson said Thursday afternoon in her office.

"There's nothing friendly about them," Erin retorted.

"The headaches are your body's way of letting tension out. We'll be detectives and try to give this friend some tangible features."

Erin thought it was a dumb idea, but rehearsals started the next afternoon, so she was desperate to do something about the headaches. "Okay. How do we start?"

"We look for a pattern. For instance, when do they occur most often?"

"No particular time." She shrugged. "They're just *there*."

"When did you have your last one?"

"Monday, after play tryouts."

"Did the tryouts go well for you?"

"I got the lead."

"Congratulations," the counselor said heartily. "But did the competing make you tense?"

"Not really," Erin answered honestly. "I've been auditioning for dance roles all my life. It's part of the fun."

"Was it easy being with the other kids? Didn't you tell me Berkshire was doing the production with you?"

"When you go to an all-girls school, being around guys is different at first. But some of them are really good-looking. Except one. His name is David, and I don't like him very much. But I'm going to have to adapt, because he got the part of Tony."

"What don't you like about him?"

"He came on too strong, I guess. He acted too friendly, sort of Mr. Personality, Life-of-the-Party, you know the type? He wasn't the one I wanted to get the part either."

"What did the others think of him?"

"Shara, my best friend, likes him. She says he's a real comedian."

"Is that when your headache started?"

"No. It was later, in the locker room. But I don't see how David could have set it off. He's more like a pain in the rear end."

Dr. Richardson laughed. "What about the headache before that? When did it come on?"

They spent some time listing what Erin could recall when each headache started. Most of the events were hazy because of the pain. Still, the pattern seemed undiscernible, and she told Dr. Richardson as much. "Don't be discouraged," the therapist said. "Something's here, we just haven't singled it out yet." Dr. Richardson studied her notes briefly. "The headaches started about a year ago, is that correct?"

"More or less. They got worse over last summer. They slacked off when school started, but they seem to be coming more often now. Since it's spring, couldn't it be allergies?" she asked hopefully.

"But you've never had allergy problems before."

"So? Allergies could explain everything. I think my parents should take me to an allergist. Don't you?"

Dr. Richardson tapped her pencil on her notepad. "We won't rule it out, but let me ask some more questions first. What happened in your life about a year ago?"

Erin knew what the therapist wanted her to say, so she chose the most direct, hard-hitting words she could. "I'm sure my parents already told you that my sister, Amy, was in a car wreck and in a coma for three weeks before she died. I'm not 'retreating from reality,' if that's what you're thinking."

"Where did you hear that phrase?"

"From one of the doctors Mom took me to in the beginning. I know that my sister's dead and nothing's going to bring her back."

Dr. Richardson frowned. "It was unfair of that doctor to make a diagnosis without a thorough evaluation. We need to look at the total person, not just body parts."

"That's the way they treated Amy," Erin said

ruefully. "There was a doctor for her brain, one for her heart, one for her other organs. They just sort of parceled her out in pieces." Erin shook her head to chase away the images of machines and monitors and antiseptic smells.

"You're telling me that you hated to see her in that condition, aren't you?"

A lump filled Erin's throat; she swallowed it down. "I know they were trying to save her life, but still it was like she was just some sort of lab experiment. I've accepted Amy's death," Erin added. "I know I won't see her again until I get to heaven. So it still doesn't make any sense for me to have the headaches."

Dr. Richardson leaned over the desk and touched Erin's shoulder. "Your heart hurts, Erin. It hurts so bad, it's making the rest of your body hurt too. The headaches may involve Amy's death, but I believe there's more to it than that."

"But what?"

"That's what we're going to find out together."

"Don't you just *love* Friday night at the mall?" Shara asked Erin as they passed in front of a plate-glass window filled with bright spring fashions. "Everybody's here."

"It's too crowded," Erin said. "If I fell down, I'd get squashed."

"Don't be negative. Maybe if you fell down, you'd get rescued."

"By whom? Have you seen some of the scuzballs hanging around this place?"

Shara let out an "Eek!" of exasperation. "Then let's count tonight as a celebration of the first rehearsal."

"It was chaos, and you know it."

"True, but it gave me plenty of time to flirt with Seth," Shara said with a dimpled smile.

"And me too much time to avoid my leading man."

"But why do you want to? David's so sweet, and he seems crazy about you."

"He's crazy, all right," Erin muttered.

"He's got a smile that lights up the stage, too," Shara insisted.

"If you think he's so terrific, then let's trade. I'll take Seth."

Shara made a face. "David doesn't know any other girl is alive. Sorry, Erin, he's absolutely zeroed in on you." Shara patted her shoulder. "Tough life, having some guy drooling at your feet."

Erin started to retort but heard someone call her name. She turned to see a girl with short reddish hair weaving her way toward her. Erin's eyes narrowed. She knew the girl but couldn't quite place her.

"It's me, Beth Clark. Remember? From the hospital last year. My mother needed a kidney transplant, and your sister was in a coma. How did it ever turn out for her?"

Chapter Four

⌒

Seeing Beth again was like seeing a ghost. For Erin she was a painful reminder of the hospital and endless days of waiting. Erin stared at her, unable to speak. Shara must have realized her friend needed rescuing, because she said, "I'm Shara Perez, Erin's friend. I used to sit with her in the waiting room."

Beth nodded. "I remember you. How's Amy?"

"She—uh—she . . ." Shara stuttered.

"She died," Erin interrupted.

Beth's face looked stricken. "Oh, I'm so sorry."

"We donated her organs."

Glancing around, Beth asked, "Would you like to go to the food court and talk?"

"Sure," Erin said, marching off swiftly in the direction of the mall's fast-food area while the others tried to keep up. Once they'd bought drinks and settled at a table, Beth said, "I'm really sorry about Amy."

"You were still in Gainesville when we had her funeral. Then later—" she shrugged and let the sentence trail. "So how's your mom doing?"

"All right. But not perfect."

"I thought that getting a new kidney would make her well."

"She still has to take medication to suppress her immune system so she won't reject the transplant. The doctors are having a hard time finding the right combination. She's depressed a lot."

Beth let her gaze wander, and Erin sensed there was a lot she was leaving out. "So, how are you doing?" Erin asked.

"As well as can be expected."

"How's that boyfriend of yours?"

"We called it quits. Between schoolwork and all the stuff I have to do at home, I didn't have much time for him."

"What stuff?" Shara asked.

Beth took a sip of her soft drink. "Taking care of my sisters and kid brother. Mom's not able to do much housework, or even cook, so I have to make sure it all gets done."

Shara grimaced. "What a drag."

"So what's going on in your life?" Beth asked, and Erin told her about the play. "Sounds exciting. I was in a play at my school last year, but I didn't have the time to go out for one this year. Who's in it from Berkshire? Maybe I know some of them."

Erin ran through several names. Shara added, "You forgot David Devlin. He's got the lead."

"David?" Beth said, breaking out into a grin. "I know him. He's *so* good! And funny too. You're going to have a ball playing opposite him." Erin held her tongue in spite of the "told-you-so" smirk

Shara gave her. Was she the only person in the universe who didn't think David was Mr. Wonderful?

Beth glanced at her watch. "I promised Mom I'd be back in an hour. It was great to see you again, Erin."

"Same here."

"Uh—maybe you could call me and remind me about the play. I'd like to see it."

Erin suddenly felt very sorry for Beth, thinking how hard it must be for her at home. Even though her family had its problems, at least *her* basic routine had remained about the same. "I'll let you know," Erin told her.

After Beth had gone, Shara asked, "Do you want to hit a few more stores?" Erin shook her head. "Are you getting a headache?"

"No," Erin said, both relieved and disappointed. On the one hand, she didn't want to face the pain, but on the other she could now be reasonably certain that her headaches had nothing to do with seeing someone who she associated with those horrible few weeks before Amy died. She made a mental note to tell Dr. Richardson. They were no closer to discovering the reason for her headaches than before.

"Quick! Duck! Devlin's got a can of slime, and he's hitting everybody!"

Seth's shout made Erin flatten herself against the wall the second she emerged from the theater's dressing room. *What now?* she wondered irritably. The rehearsal had gone well, but now that everyone was supposed to be getting ready to leave, David was pulling a stupid prank.

She heard kids giggling and saw Shara slip behind a partially painted flat with Seth. Erin calculated the fastest route to the outside stage door and away from the dumb game. She inched along the wall, spied the door, and prepared to make a dash for it. Suddenly all the lights went out.

Erin froze, hearing muffled screeches and kids banging into chairs and props. Someone yelled, "You're dead meat, Devlin!"

Erin crouched, trying hard to remember the path to the door. An arm shot around her waist and pulled her close against a warm body. A melodramatic voice rasped in her ear, "Now you're mine, my pretty!"

"David!"

"Shh," he warned. "Don't give away our position."

"Don't you dare slime me," Erin hissed.

"What? I'd sooner deface the Sistine Chapel. No, you're my hostage."

"Let go of me!"

"Can't," David whispered. "Seth and Andy have cans of slime too. It's them against us now."

"I don't want to play."

David seized her hand and pulled her behind him. "Too late. If they see you with me, you'll get slimed for sure."

From the far side of the stage, Andy yelled, "Pinky, turn the lights on."

Great, Erin thought. Everybody was involved

in the foolishness. She tried to tug away from David, but his grip was tight. "In here," he said, pulling her down into a large wooden box.

"Where are we?" she asked.

"Prop box," David said. "I cased it out when I got here tonight. They'll never find us in here."

"You mean you *planned* this?"

"Of course. The cast needs to lighten up and have some fun. And so do you."

"Ms. Thornton and Mr. Ault will have an attack."

"What are they gonna do, fire us?"

Erin knew he was grinning, even though she couldn't see his face. "I don't want to be here with you," she said, hoping to sound icy.

"So where would you rather be with me? Just name it."

Outside, Pinky shouted, "I found the lights!" The lid of the prop box was closed, so Erin saw only a small stream of light through a crack. Andy called, "Come on out, Devlin. I promise to make this as painful as possible."

David scrunched lower and, not knowing why, Erin ducked in tighter next to him. She could tell by the sound of Andy's voice that he was standing right outside the box. Her heart pounded and she held her breath.

Next to her, David coiled. He dropped her hand. She sensed what he was going to do and pulled to one side. With a rebel yell, David flipped up the top of the box, stood, and sprayed a startled Andy directly in the face.

"He slimed me!" Andy wailed.

Erin peeked over the edge of the box in time to see five kids emerge from the shadows and surround David, who skidded to a halt.

"We've got him now," Seth said. "Tighten the ranks," he ordered. Shara, Pinky, and three boys locked arms and slowly closed inward.

David shook his can of slime and shrugged. "Gee fellas, I'm all out," he said.

"Prepare to *die*, alien," Seth said.

Erin climbed out of the box, wide-eyed, torn between wanting to see David get his just rewards and wanting to see him outwit his friends one final time. Seth hit the nozzle as David did an elaborate pratfall. The movement was so quick, so well timed, and so effortless, that no one saw it coming. The slime spewed across the small circle and doused Shara and Pinky, while David rolled like an acrobat, sprang to his feet, and darted away.

Erin felt struck by déjà vu as an image of a similar pratfall flashed through her mind. She struggled to bring the memory into focus, but it eluded her like mist, and the screaming and laughing around her pushed the memory even further out of reach.

Soon everyone scattered, still laughing and talking, to clean off the messy slime. Erin, haunted by David's pratfall, heard him organizing a trip to McDonald's. "Hey, Erin, can you come with us?"

A hard knot of tension was forming at the base of her neck. "I—I can't."

He walked over to her. "Are you mad?" he asked.

"No. I just can't come tonight."

"Maybe next time?" Erin started to feel desperate to get away. Shara walked past, and David caught her arm. "Can you persuade Erin to come with us?"

Shara questioned Erin with her eyes. The knot was growing, and Erin felt the tightness inching up her skull. She had to get out of there fast and drive home while she still could. She kneaded the back of her neck, hoping Shara would get the message. "I really can't," she said.

Shara understood. She tucked her arm through David's and said, "Oh no you don't, wise guy. You're not going to stand here flirting with Erin while the rest of us clean up this mess. Come on."

Erin quickly gathered her things and left. Somehow she made it home, where she took her headache medication and crawled into bed. Nausea made her gag, and she writhed on the cool sheets praying for the pain to go away. But every time she closed her eyes, the image of David's pratfall replayed in her mind.

She didn't know why. She couldn't explain it. Yet she was completely and absolutely convinced that somehow David Devlin was mixed up in the headache's arrival.

Chapter Five

~

"You want me to pull David from the cast, and you won't even tell me why? Erin, that makes no sense."

Erin tugged at the leg of her leotard and avoided eye contact with Ms. Thornton. "I don't mean to cause problems. It's just that I—uh—I don't get along with him too well."

"Artistic differences? Come on now—he's an excellent actor, and you're much too professional to be pitching a temper tantrum."

Erin couldn't stand for Ms. Thornton to think badly of her. In spite of her being a teacher, their relationship was more like a friendship; yet she couldn't run the risk of being around David and having another headache either. What if one came on during the actual performance?

Ms. Thornton's eyes narrowed. "He didn't try something with you, did he? I mean, it's obvious he's smitten, but is he harassing you?"

"Oh no. Please, that's not it at all."

Ms. Thornton reached out and took Erin's arm. "What is it then? Tell me. I want to help."

Erin caught the reflections of the dancers'

bodies dressed in contrasting leotards and tights in the wall of mirrors, and she wished the floor would open up and swallow her. How could she tell Ms. Thornton the truth? Maybe she'd decide to replace *her* instead of David. "It—it's nothing. He sort of gets on my nerves, that's all."

"Hardly a reason to drop him from the play," Ms. Thornton said. "You know, Erin, you're the best student I've ever had, and you have a wonderful sense of professionalism. You have a future in this business, and you'll often have to work with people you aren't nuts about. You may as well learn how to do it now."

Erin felt silly and foolish. "Forget I said anything."

"It's forgotten," Ms. Thornton said, smiling. "In fact, Mr. Ault is working with David privately to bone up his dance numbers. He has a decent voice, so we'll let him record his song numbers on cassette for playback in the actual performances. In fact"— the teacher paused and measured Erin in the mirror—"I've been considering asking you to work extra with him too. In light of our discussion, will that be a problem?"

Erin's heart sank. "Of course not. I'm a professional, remember?"

Ms. Thornton grew serious. "Look, honey, I know it's been a tough year for you, but you seem to be doing well. Are you?"

"Um—all right. Some days are better than others." No use pretending to Ms. Thornton that her life was a bed of roses, but no sense in dumping the whole truth on her either.

"I want you to think again about taking that Wolftrap scholarship this summer. The offer's still open."

Erin was half-afraid it would be. She wanted it, but if the headaches didn't go away, if Dr. Richardson couldn't help her discover the cause . . . She faked a bright smile. "Let's see how I do with this play. I mean, if David and I don't kill each other before it's over."

Ms. Thornton smiled. "You'll figure out a way to get along with him. He *is* kind of cute," she added. "And he's certainly attracted to you."

Erin rolled her eyes. "That's the last thing I need."

"Or the first," Ms. Thornton said, then began doing leg lifts on the bar while Erin stared blankly in the mirror.

Erin found her mother in the garage sorting laundry. "Um—have you see any metal chain out here?" she asked.

"All I'm seeing is a week's worth of dirty clothes," her mother complained. "What do you need a chain for?"

"It's for the rumble scene in the play—the big gang fight."

"This place is such a mess, you'll be lucky to find anything."

Erin glanced around at the piles of junk, heavy

with dust and grime. "Looks like we need another family workday. We haven't had one of those in"— she wrinkled her brow—"way over a year."

"No one has time anymore to do anything around here."

"I could make the time," Erin said quickly, seeing it as an opportunity for them to do something together as a family. So what if it was grungy, dirty work? At least it would bring them together for a day.

"I'm swamped at the boutique, and I know your father won't take his nose out of his books long enough to do anything as mundane as garage cleanup."

Erin hadn't counted on her mother's animosity toward her father. She was suddenly sick and tired of all their hassling. "What's the matter with you two? Do you always have to be at war with each other?"

Mrs. Bennett shoved a load of laundry into the machine. "You couldn't possibly understand—"

"Is it me? Is it something I've done to make you both angry?"

"Oh, of course not, darling. You're all we have." The tears brimming in her mother's eyes shocked Erin. She hadn't meant to make her cry. "Why if it weren't for you—" Her mother's sentence trailed, and Erin felt panicked. If it weren't for her what? Would her parents break up? Mrs. Bennett grabbed her, hugging her fiercely. "Don't you see? You're all that's left. I—I can't stand the thought of losing you."

"You won't, Mom," Erin mumbled, confused and a little scared by her mother's wide emotional swing from anger at her husband to clingy tearfulness over her daughter. And what did she mean about "losing" her? She was moving away to college next year. They'd discussed it many times. If only Amy were still with them, then perhaps it would be easier to leave. Amy was *supposed* to have been at home another year.

Awkwardly Erin broke free and skirted her father's overloaded workbench. "I—uh—I have to find that chain."

She searched hurriedly, eager to get away. Suddenly she saw it on a stack of boxes next to an old trunk against the cement block wall. The black lettering had faded, but each container was marked "Amy" in her father's neat writing.

"What's wrong?" her mother asked from across the garage. "Did you find it?"

"Yes," she said, unable to take her eyes off the boxes and trunk. She remembered the day her parents had cleaned out Amy's room and packed away the total accumulation of her sixteen years on planet Earth.

"You should go through this stuff," her mother had said through her tears. "There'll be things you'll want to keep."

"Not now," Erin had told her. "Maybe someday."

Her father had taped each box shut, and her mother had wept, "My baby, my poor baby."

"That won't help, Marian," her father had admonished. "We have to get on with life, and crying about Amy won't bring her back."

Erin blinked, and the vivid pictures from the past faded to the dingy darkness of the garage. She grabbed the chain, dragged it toward the washer and dryer, and stuffed it into a paper sack. "Ugh, it's all rusty. You'd better wash up in the laundry sink," her mother said.

Erin stared at the rust that had stained her hands brown. She quickly washed them, watching in macabre fascination as soap and water cleaned away the red brown stain that reminded her of dried blood.

David was late for their special rehearsal with Mr. Ault, and Erin grew angrier by the second. She adjusted her leg warmers and did several arabesques in the center of the stage before asking, "Where is he? We've been waiting twenty minutes, and I told my mom I'd work at her store this afternoon."

Mr. Ault shrugged. "David's never been punctual. I'll have to remind him again that we must start on time."

They heard the outside stage door bang, and seconds later David bounded across the stage and skidded to a halt, saying, "Sorry," and flashing a boyish grin.

"Well, it's about time," Erin mumbled.

"It was my sister's birthday, and I had to do my bit."

"You have a sister?"

"Yeah. Jody. She turned eight today."

"Let's get started," Mr. Ault said, cuing up the cassette for the musical number during which Tony and Maria meet at the neighborhood dance amid the rivaling gangs. "This is slow. The rest of the cast is frozen in motion, the lights dim, the spot comes up and pulls Tony and Maria to the center of the stage. They look with wonder at each other and then . . ." He put Erin's hand in David's and made them face one another.

David's fingers felt warm. Since he wasn't tall, she only had to raise her chin slightly to look him in the eye. "I'll try not to damage your feet," he told her.

"I only dance on the bottoms," she said, hoping a little humor would relax her.

David turned on his famous megawatt smile. She noticed a white substance smeared along his jawline and squinted at it. "What's wrong?" he asked.

"There's some kind of white stuff on your neck."

He dropped her hand and wiped his face. "Greasepaint. I thought I got it all off."

She wondered why he'd been wearing white greasepaint but didn't want to ask. *No use getting too friendly*, she thought. They danced for a few minutes to Mr. Ault's instructions. David was amazingly light on his feet and a quick learner.

He pulled her closer, and she rested her cheek on his shoulder, all the while keeping pace to the music. He was muscular and solid and smelled like sunshine.

"That's good," Mr. Ault said. "Remember, you two are beginning to fall in love here. . . . No, Erin, don't stiffen. Relax. That's better. Now, 'Tony,' spin her slowly, push her outward . . . pull her back . . . yes, very good. Now stop dancing and act like you're about to kiss her."

David's face dipped lower. Erin's heart began to hammer. When his mouth was inches from hers, Mr. Ault said, "Hold it. Perfect. Now, at this point Tony and Maria will freeze, the spotlight will widen, the lights will come up, and the others will dance around them."

Erin scarcely heard him, because David's mouth was coming closer. By reflex her eyes closed and her chin tilted, and David's lips brushed over hers. The contact jolted Erin out of her trance. Her eyelids opened wide; she brought up her palms and shoved hard against David's chest. "Don't do that!" she cried.

"What's the problem?" Mr. Ault groaned. "It was going so well."

David staggered backwards, throwing up his hands in innocence. "My mouth slipped," he explained.

"You're not supposed to kiss her here, hot lips," Mr. Ault said. "Not until act three."

"He's such a pain!"

"Come on, Erin," the teacher admonished. "Let's try to be professional. David, back off."

Erin squeezed her eyes shut, afraid she was

going to cry. Why *was* she overreacting? She felt a throbbing and a tightening in her temples. How was she ever going to make it till the play opened in six weeks? "This is just supposed to be for blocking out the dance moves," she said. "He—he caught me off guard, that's all."

"Can we try it again?" Mr. Ault asked. "And this time, David, keep your lips from 'slipping.'"

David saluted and took Erin in his arms again. "Loosen up," he said. "It was just a kiss."

Erin glared at him. They made it through the number several more times, and when Mr. Ault was finally pleased and had dismissed them, Erin hurried to get her things, because the pressure in her skull was building. At the stage door David stopped her before she could get outside. His expression was serious and contemplative. "Why don't you like me?" he asked.

Erin tried to shrug him off. "You surprised me, that's all."

"I don't think so. You haven't liked me since day one."

"I—it isn't personal."

"How else can it be? You don't even know me. We've never even met before."

Something about him nagged at the back of her mind. "I'm sorry. Really." She seemed to be saying that phrase a lot lately.

David tipped his head to one side, and his eyes gleamed with mischief. "Would you like me more if I gave you a present?"

"I don't want anything. I have to go." She tried

to step around him, but he dodged in front of her, pulled a balloon from his pocket, and proceeded to blow it up.

"I'm really a nice guy," he said between puffs of air. "Kids and dogs are nuts about me. I'm gonna make you a dachshund out of this balloon to prove it." He twisted the balloon into shape. "Don't look so surprised. See, at heart, I'm really a clown."

In that instant Erin knew exactly where she'd seen David Devlin before.

Chapter Six

"You didn't recognize him until he said the word 'clown'?" Dr. Richardson asked, tapping her pencil on the side of her notepad. "Why not?"

"The first time we met, we were both wearing full clown makeup. White greasepaint, fake noses, wigs, big sloppy costumes—there's no way I could have known who he was when he auditioned for the play. When we performed at the Children's Home together last Easter, I didn't even know his last name." Erin was relieved and elated that she'd solved the mystery of why David made her feel uncomfortable. "I guess that I disliked him because he reminds me of when Amy was in the hospital."

"A lot of things must remind you of Amy. But not everything that reminds you gives you a headache."

Erin fidgeted in the chair. She was so sure she'd hit on the solution to her headaches generated by David. "I was just making an observation," she said testily.

"Did you tell David about meeting him before?"

"Oh, no," Erin said. "I don't want him to know."

"Why?"

"I'd feel stupid talking about it. He didn't know Amy. And I'll never be a clown again. So why bring it up?"

Dr. Richardson pushed away from her desk and sat back in her chair. "Do you know what a support group is, Erin?"

"It's a group of people who have something in common. There's a support group at Briarwood for girls with divorced parents, and they meet once a week."

"I oversee a grief support group for young people who've lost a parent or a sibling or even a friend."

"So?"

"I'd like you to meet with us."

"I meet with *you*."

"You'd continue to meet with me, but you'd also meet with them. We gather in my conference room on Friday nights."

"I don't think so."

"Why?"

"I'm pretty busy already. Between school and dance classes and now the play, I don't have much free time. If I have any, I work in Mom's store."

"You could make time."

"I really don't want to come." Dr. Richardson looked at her expectantly, so Erin continued. "I don't want to sit around with a bunch of strangers and talk about Amy."

"Talking often helps—both you and the others. It helps you realize that you're not alone, that other people have been through the same thing and feel similar emotions."

"No one feels like I do. And talking won't bring Amy back."

"But facing your feelings can help *you*."

Erin wanted to scream. Why did the counselor keep firing dumb suggestions at her? "Look, I need to cut today short. I've got lots of homework tonight." She stood. "I thought you'd be glad that I figured out why I didn't like David."

"I'm not sure that's all of it."

"What do you mean?"

"I think there's a deeper reason why you feel uncomfortable around this boy."

"Like what?"

"We're looking for the answers together, aren't we?"

"In other words, you want me to figure it out on my own," Erin said. If Dr. Richardson knew what was wrong, why wouldn't she tell her?

"Please consider coming to the support group."

"I said I was too busy." She stood and crossed to the door. "I've got play practice too, so I gotta go now."

The therapist picked up her appointment pad. "I'll put you down for next week," she said.

Erin nodded, but deep down she doubted she'd make the appointment. She was tired of talking about the past, and so far nothing much had changed. She still got headaches. And now, with the counselor pressuring her to come and spill her guts in front of a bunch of strangers . . . Why would she talk to strangers about things she couldn't even discuss with her own parents?

Friday night after rehearsal some of the cast went out for pizza, and Shara all but dragged Erin along. At the pizza parlor six of them squeezed into a booth. Wedged between David and Andy, Erin grimaced at Shara on the other side of the dimly lit table. The aroma of tomato sauce and cheese made Erin's stomach growl. "And you said you weren't hungry," David joked.

"I said I didn't want to come," Erin corrected. A part of Erin really wanted to be there, but a part of her felt cut off and distanced from the others. It made no sense to her. "I've got to work at my mom's boutique tomorrow."

"So what?" Seth asked. "Do you turn into a pumpkin at midnight?"

The others laughed, and Erin felt her face flush.

"I've got a show to do, but I can't let a small detail like being up at seven A.M. deter me from pizza," David offered, drawing the attention away from Erin.

"Where?" Seth wanted to know. "Maybe we'll drop by and throw tomatoes."

David flipped water on him from his water glass. "I wouldn't notice even if you did. I don't actually wake up until noon. Just ask my science teacher," he joked.

"Lots of fun things come in the morning," Pinky told him.

"Name three."

"Santa Claus," said Shara quickly.

"The Tooth Fairy," Andy added.

"Unconfirmed," David told him. "Many suspect she comes late at night."

"Sunrise," Erin said quietly, remembering how Amy used to hate getting up in the mornings too. "Sunrise comes early in the morning." The others looked at her oddly. *How could I say such a stupid thing?* she thought.

"That can be confirmed," David interjected hastily, as if to cover for her.

Seth cleared his throat, and the awkward moment passed when the waitress brought a pizza, still sizzling from the oven. David divided up the pie and continued with a string of stories that kept the others laughing

Erin half listened, concentrating instead on picking the mushrooms off her slice of pizza. She flicked them absently, wondering where her hunger had gone. Her stomach was kntted for some reason, and she just couldn't eat.

"Something wrong with the food?" David asked.

"I'm just not a mushroom fanatic."

"Not a mushroom fanatic!" David feigned horror. "But mushrooms are our friends. In fact some of my best friends are mushrooms. Consider Seth here. . . ."

A tiny smile curled Erin's lip as David quickly started another conversation, this time about basketball. David did have the gift of charm and a ready wit, something she'd always envied in people. Amy had been that way, she thought. She set her piece of pizza down and tuned into what Andy was saying. ". . . no way, Devlin. You've got your hopes pinned on the wrong team. The Celtics are gonna take it all."

"In your dreams, buddy. How could you ever pick the Celtics to come out on top? Get with it, man! You'd have to be brain dead to pick them."

For Erin the world seemed to stop spinning, and the walls of the room closed in on her. *Brain dead.* She stood rapidly, pushing Andy out of the booth.

"Hey!" he yelped.

Erin didn't care. She only knew she had to get out of there before she screamed. She felt as if she were running through a thick fog. She heard Shara shout, "Erin! Wait!" She even felt a hand grab at her. But she wrenched away and ran to the door. People were staring, but it didn't matter. She had to get outside and into the cool night air.

She ran across the parking lot to her car and dug frantically through her purse. *Where are the stupid keys?* She climbed into the front seat and spilled the contents of her purse in her lap. She found them, finally, and jammed one into the ignition. She never got to turn it, though, because someone yanked open the passenger door, jumped in, and tugged the key from the switch.

Erin turned furiously toward the intruder, David Devlin. "Go away!" she shouted. "Go away and leave me alone!"

Chapter Seven

"I mean it," Erin said through clenched teeth. In the light from the overhead street lamp, she saw David's tortured expression.

"I'm sorry, Erin. I—I didn't know."

"Didn't know what? Give me my keys."

"I didn't know that you had a sister who died."

"Who told you?" Her chin lifted defiantly.

"Shara did, the minute you ran out. All I heard her say was that your sister had been brain dead after a car wreck; then I ran out after you."

"Shara's got a big mouth. The truth is I'm sick to my stomach."

David reached for her, and she shoved him away. "My keys." She held out her open palm.

"Talk to me," he pleaded. "Tell me what happened."

"If you don't give me my keys and get out of this car, I'm going to start screaming." Her hands were shaking, and tears were straining behind her eyes. Why didn't he go away and leave her alone?

"No," David said.

She lunged. He tossed the keys into the backseat and grabbed her wrists and pulled her toward him. She struggled to break free, fought to hold back the tears, but she couldn't do either. With a strangled cry the dam broke.

David held her, and she didn't resist because the fight had gone out of her. She didn't know how long she wept, but eventually the tears subsided, leaving her as limp as a rag doll. She fumbled in her lap for a tissue, while David stroked her hair. She eased back into her seat, but David held tightly to her right hand. "I haven't cried like that since . . ." Her voice sounded raspy. She remembered the day that her parents had signed the organ-donor papers for Amy and she'd stood in the shower wearing all her clothes and cried. ". . . well, for a long time." She was embarrassed, because no one had ever seen her lose it that way.

"Are you still mad at me?" David asked.

"No, you had no way of knowing."

David took a deep breath. "I wouldn't have hurt you for the world, Erin. My dad always tells me that I talk too much."

"It doesn't matter." Outside, people drove cars out of the lot, but Erin felt isolated and alone with David, as if they were the only two people in the world. She rolled down her window, and the night air cooled her hot, tearstained cheeks.

"Tell me about your sister," David said. "What was her name?"

"Amy," Erin told him. It seemed strange that he didn't know. For years everybody she'd known had known Amy too. "She was sixteen, a sophomore at Briarwood."

"You must miss her a lot."

Fresh tears came up, but Erin blinked them away. "Yes." David reached out and ran his thumb across her cheek. "I must look awful," she said, sorting through the mess in her lap for her hairbrush.

"Not to me." Without warning her heart began to thud. She glanced at him shyly. He took her hand. "I think you're beautiful."

She shrugged self-consciously. "You didn't get to eat your pizza."

"I don't like mushrooms either."

All at once David seemed different to her, kind and caring, not crazy and foolish. She was ashamed that she'd judged him before getting to know him. "I'd better get this stuff put away. I really do have to get home."

"I'll help." He held the purse while she scooped her belongings into it. "What time do you have to be at work tomorrow?" he asked.

"Not until three o'clock," she said, embarrassed that inside the pizza parlor she'd made it sound much earlier than that.

"Good." David reached over into the backseat and hunted for her keys. "I'll pick you up at ten."

"What? But—but—"

"No 'buts.'" He handed her the keys and opened the car door.

"But where are we going?"

"I have a show to do, and I want you with me. And I want to introduce you to the second-most-important woman in my life."

"Who . . . ?"

David got out. "Tomorrow," he said, shutting the door and jogging back to the restaurant.

"But . . ." Erin said to the empty car. Slowly, thoughtfully, she started the engine and pulled out into the light flow of traffic. "The *second*-most-important woman?" she asked aloud. Did that make her the first? Erin smiled despite her confusion over David.

That night she lay in her bed and remembered how gentle he'd been with her, how he'd let her cry herself out, holding her and hugging her. She noted something else too. For the first time in months, she felt peaceful, as if the tears had washed away the hard knots that lived inside her stomach and along her spine. And she also realized that she'd told him about Amy and didn't have a headache.

"Couldn't you have put your makeup on when you got there?" Erin asked, staring at David as he drove, dressed in his full clown gear.

"It's a kid's birthday party," he said. "Can't spoil the illusion by going off to the bathroom and changing when I get there, can I?" He looked over at her and grinned. Even under the white greasepaint and big orange mouth, she recognized his electric smile. He looked exactly as he had a year ago—oversize baggy suit, yellow curly wig, and bowler hat perched on his head. A flower she knew squirted water was stuck in his lapel.

"People are staring," Erin said as a car passed them and the driver did a double take.

David waved. "That's the trouble with the world. It's too conventional."

David might be indifferent to what others thought, but Erin wasn't. It was one of the things that made her and Amy so different. Amy never cared what others thought, while to Erin it had always mattered. Maybe that's why Amy, and now David, made friends so easily; and why it had been so out of character for Erin to dress in Amy's clown makeup the year before and fulfill Amy's commitment at the Children's Home. "People hardly expect to see a clown driving down the freeway," Erin told him.

"Careful, sweet-face, or I'll douse you with water. But then, I don't want to spoil my routine for you."

Erin almost told him that she knew his routine but decided that it would take too much explaining. "So who's this all-important woman I'm supposed to meet?"

"She's a regular doll," he said mysteriously. "You'll love her."

Erin wasn't too sure. David parked his car in front of a two-story brick house on a tree-lined side street off Bayshore Drive. She could smell the salt water in the breeze. He took Erin's hand and led her up the sloped driveway. The door of the side entrance flew open, and a little girl with blue eyes and dark blond hair barreled out and grabbed David around the waist.

"Whoa," he said, laughing and hugging her. She made several gestures with her hands, and

David responded with rapid gestures as well as words. "I know I'm late, but I told you I had to pick up a friend."

The girl turned toward Erin who watched, fascinated as the child's fingers flew in more gestures and signs. "This is Erin," David said, shaping her name with his fingers. "We're in the play at school together."

The girl measured Erin with wide, unblinking eyes. Caught off guard, Erin didn't know how to respond. "This is my sister, Jody," David said.

Erin was at a momentary loss. Why hadn't David told her that his sister was deaf? "I—um—hello, Jody."

"Watch," David told her. "This is the sign for 'Hello.'"

Erin repeated it awkwardly, and Jody giggled, then turned back to David and signed something. David laughed. "She thinks you're pretty," he told Erin. "And she wants to know how I got such a pretty girl to date *me*."

Just then a woman flung open the screen and ushered the three of them inside a big, sunlit kitchen. "David, the kids are waiting for you in the den."

"Well, I can't keep my public waiting, can I?"

Twenty children sat on the floor in a semicircle, and they giggled and pointed when David entered. Erin hung toward the back of the room, where she watched as David performed. He did magic tricks, made animal shapes out of balloons, and managed a few pratfalls in between. Watching

him, Erin felt her throat grow thick. She kept remembering how well they'd worked together at the
Children's Home, and she couldn't understand why
she hadn't told him about it before now. She felt
that she was deceiving him in some way.

"Isn't he wonderful?" the mother of the birthday child whispered in Erin's ear.

"Yes," Erin said.

"We've known his family for years. My daughter, Tracy, and David's sister, Jody, started at the
same school for the hearing impaired when they
were both two."

"That young?" For the first time Erin per-
ceived that in spite of all the laughter, the room was
strangely quiet to be filled with twenty children.
"Are all these kids deaf?"

"That term's inaccurate," Tracy's mother said.
"Some are more handicapped than others. Tracy
and Jody both are considered 'profoundly deaf'—
they can't hear anything. Others have some hearing
with the use of special hearing aids. They all attend
a special school where they're taught a combination
of signing and lipreading. They're all taught to talk
too, but since speaking depends so much on hearing, they don't sound like regular kids to the rest of
us."

"In other words, you can't imitate what you
can't hear?" Erin asked.

"That's right. Eventually we want to main-
stream Tracy and Jody."

Erin knew that mainstreaming meant putting

kids with handicaps into regular classrooms. "Was Jody born deaf?" she asked.

"No. When she was a year old, she caught meningitis, and it left her without her hearing."

"She's a pretty girl."

"Yes, and she absolutely adores her big brother. He's a nice guy and very talented."

Erin watched as David brought Tracy from the audience and made quarters appear from behind her ears. Then he presented her with a bouquet of flowers that seemingly materialized from under his coat.

When it was time to serve the cake, Erin helped Tracy's mom pass it among the children, then she and David slipped out the back door. In the car David tugged off his hat and wig and red false nose and tossed them to the backseat.

"I'm impressed," Erin said. "You had them eating out of your hand."

He grinned, and his orange-painted mouth stretched cheek to cheek. "All women under the age of ten fall at my feet."

"It must be your humility that attracts them."

David snickered. "That's one of the reasons I keep you around, Erin. You never let me forget I'm a mere mortal."

"*Someone* has to remind you."

They rode in contented silence for awhile. "How about a Coke?" David asked.

"Sounds good. You look like you could use one too. Your face is running."

David laughed and swiped at the greasepaint with a tissue. It smeared, making his dark-penciled eyebrows smudge over his forehead. He turned into the driveway of a McDonald's and parked.

"You're not going to drive through?" Erin asked incredulously.

David got out of the car, came around, opened her door, and offered her his hand. "Why?"

"Well because—I mean—your makeup and all. People will stare."

"Stop caring what people think, Erin. Life's too short to live it by other people's rules. Come on, let's go in." Still she hesitated. He held out his hand and added, "If you do, I'll be your best friend."

Erin felt as if a giant hand had clutched her heart. "Why did you say that?" she asked, her voice trembling. "Why did you say that to me?"

Chapter Eight

∽

"What did I say?" David asked.

For a moment Erin couldn't get it out. "'I'll be your best friend,'" she finally said.

They were standing in the middle of McDonald's, in everyone's way. "Let's sit down, all right?" David led her to a booth in the back.

Erin slid across the vinyl, another knot forming in her stomach.

"Now what's wrong with being best friends?" David asked.

"It—it was just something my sister used to say all the time."

David shook his head and sighed. "I have no way of knowing these things, Erin, and I hate having to be on my guard around you all the time. I probably picked it up from the kids—they say that all the time."

His attitude irked her. She at least wanted him to be sorry. "Can I have that Coke now?"

While David ordered, Erin stared pensively out of the window, wondering about her feelings toward him. Sometimes he got on her nerves, yet other times he seemed so sensitive and kind.

When he returned, she saw that he'd been to the men's room and removed the greasepaint. *Chalk one up to sensitivity,* she told herself. "So how did you ever get into clowning?" Erin asked, attempting to lift the cloud that had fallen between them.

David sat across from her. "My mom tells me I was born a comedian. Anyway, after Jody was diagnosed as deaf, I noticed that her eyes always followed me whenever we were in a room together. I used to make gestures and faces to make her smile."

"She does have a pretty smile." Pretty smiles seemed to run in his family, though Erin didn't want to tell him that.

"Thanks. When Jody started at the special school, our family learned how to sign so that we could communicate with her. When she was little, she'd throw terrible tantrums if we didn't understand her. We couldn't let her get away with it, but I understood how frustrating it was for her when no one could figure out what she was trying to say."

Erin knew what he meant. She'd been the only one to understand Amy's baby babble when they'd been small. "So you became her interpreter?" Erin asked.

"That's right. My parents would ask, 'David, what's she saying?' Anyway, I began to pantomime and entertain her. And one thing led to another until I had such a routine down, that I began performing at birthday parties and hospitals to make extra money."

"Is that why you've decided to become an actor?"

"Partly. You know, deep down clowns are really serious people. They see the good and bad in life and help people laugh about both."

"But sometimes there's nothing funny about life."

David shrugged. "Not to me. I think that hurting gives us a way to measure being happy. How can you know one without knowing the other? It's the difference between doing a hard dance move and an easy one. Which would you rather do?"

"The hard one's more challenging, so I feel better if I do it well."

"That's the way I feel about life. Why walk around desensitized? Why go for the easy moves when the hard ones make you feel better? I watch Jody deal with other peoples' ignorance every day. People who don't understand her handicap and who laugh at her whenever she tries to talk because she sounds weird to them. Sometimes it gets her down, but most of the time she keeps right on going." David balled the wrapper from his straw and bounced it on the tabletop. "I decided that making people laugh is sort of my mission in life. So I do my clown bit whenever I can. I'm doing the Special Olympics in June."

"Isn't that when all the handicapped kids compete in sports events out at USF?"

"Yes. Jody and some of her friends are competing. The organizers are always looking for people to help with the events." David snapped his fingers and added, "Say, maybe you'd like to help out! You know, if you have the time."

An image of Amy surrounded by machines and hoses, and with tubes sticking out of her mouth and arms, caused Erin to recoil. She couldn't face spending the day around kids who looked imperfect. Yet there was no way she could tell that to David. "I—I don't know. June's a long way off. We still have the play to get through."

"Speaking of the play, are you really going to make me meet you at the theater Monday morning at seven to practice our dance moves?"

"Absolutely."

David groaned and dropped his forehead dramatically against the table. "I can barely walk that time of the day, much less dance. Are you always such a slave driver?"

Erin recalled how Amy always groaned about getting up early. "I'm going to college to study dance theory, so I need to spend a lot of time practicing if I'm going to be good. Don't you practice so you can get better?"

"I practice," David said, his blue eyes holding hers. "But I never forget that it's supposed to be fun."

"And you think I do?"

"I think you need to loosen up and not take things so seriously."

"Life *is* serious," she countered. "And it can sometimes be too short."

"That's the point." David took her hand, lacing

his fingers through hers. "If it *is* short, shouldn't you have some good times along the way? Shouldn't you give everything you can to the people you meet?"

Erin pulled away, because a tightness was beginning to crawl up her back into the base of her skull. "I have to be at my mom's store soon. We'd better go."

David studied her so openly that Erin began to squirm. At last he said, "We clowns make people laugh and forget about their problems. The strange part is that whenever we do, we forget about our own problems. So, I'm going to see to it that you lighten up and let yourself go if it takes the rest of the school year."

"You do that," Erin said, standing because of the tightness that was inching slowly into her temples. David didn't understand, and she could never describe to him what it was like to have someone close to you die; to have a family of four suddenly become a family of three, and to feel like a sole survivor—a leftover that parents fight about.

"Are you going to Spring Fling?" Shara lay on Erin's bedroom floor tossing raisins into the air and trying to catch them in her mouth.

"When is it?" Erin asked.

"After spring break because Easter comes so late. You missed it last year, and since we're seniors, this'll be our last opportunity to go."

"I missed it because that was the day my folks

had decided to donate Amy's organs to medical science, and I couldn't hack the idea."

A hundred unspoken things passed between the two girls, but Erin couldn't bring herself to discuss any of them. Her fight with Travis after he'd taken Cindy Pitzer to the big formal dance stood out most vividly in Erin's mind.

Shara cleared her throat. "Well I think you should come this year."

"Who are you going with?"

"I've already asked Seth. Why don't you ask David so we can double?"

"David!"

Shara sat up. "Why not? You two are getting along better. I can tell by the way you act toward him at play practices."

"'Getting along better' doesn't mean I want to date the guy."

"For crying out loud, you're not gonna *marry* him. It's just a dance, and we could have a lot of fun double-dating. Don't be a party pooper."

Erin stretched, grabbed her toes, and bent to touch her forehead to her knees. It was true that ever since last Saturday she had been friendlier to David—in spite of the fact that he'd stuffed a toy snake into her duffel bag, and when she'd unzipped it, the snake had sprung out and almost given her heart failure. Yet he'd also stuck a rosebud under the windshield wiper on her car. There was no predicting what David was going to do.

"I don't know, Shara. I don't want to encourage

him. It's just another month until the play, and then I won't see him anymore."

"It doesn't have to be that way. You could date him until you go off to college."

If my parents let me go off to college, Erin thought. She and her mother had had another fight about it the other day when Erin couldn't work because of a headache. "I don't want to start anything with David."

"One dance," Shara pleaded. "We can go shopping for new dresses, then on the night of the dance make them take us to dinner—we can even stay out all night. Come on, it's our last big blowout before graduation."

Erin felt herself wavering. While David wasn't her ideal choice for a lasting memory of high school prom night, it might be the last time she got to do something like that with Shara. They *were* best friends, and they had gone to the Fling as sophomores and had had a blast. Yet so much had happened to her since that carefree sophomore year. Erin wondered if she'd ever feel that way again. "I'll think about it," she told Shara.

"Good." Her friend's face broke into a smile. "Then all we have to get through is the play and finals. After that"—Shara snapped her fingers—"we're off to college and the real world."

Erin agreed with a smile she didn't feel. Didn't Shara understand that Erin already had been thrust into the "real world" the day Amy died and the doctors harvested her organs for transplantation? "Do you want to her my newest tape?" Erin asked, changing the subject.

"I would, but I gotta go. I told Mom I'd clean my room today. She threatened to ground me if I don't."

Erin surveyed her bedroom. Everything was in order. She wondered why she was so fastidiously neat when most of her friends weren't. "I've been gone so much, I haven't been around to mess it up," she said, feeling as if she should defend her tidiness.

"You're the perfect daughter, Erin," Shara said. "My mother would *kill* to have me as organized as you. But I never will be. I'm messy, and I don't care."

After Shara had gone, Erin traced a path around her room, absently studying her belongings. The dance posters, the paraphernalia that she'd collected through the years, had once meant so much to her. Now she wasn't so sure. When had it changed? When had it stopped being important and started being just a bunch of old stuff?

The phone on her bureau rang, startling her. She grabbed the receiver.

"Erin?" The girl's voice on the other end sounded quiet and breathy.

"Who's this?"

"It's me, Beth Clark. Oh, Erin, could you meet me at the mall? If I don't get out of my house, I'm gonna go nuts."

Chapter Nine

Erin met Beth at the food court in the mall, where they bought Cokes and sat in cold metal chairs under pink-striped umbrellas. Beth looked thinner to Erin, and there were dark circles under her eyes. "Thanks for coming," Beth said.

"No problem. What's up? You sounded desperate."

"I *am* desperate. I don't think I can stand it for one more day in my house."

Shocked, Erin asked, "What's wrong?"

"It looks like my mom's kidney is failing."

"The transplant?"

"Yes," Beth said miserably.

"What happens if it does?"

"They have to find another donor."

"Gee, Beth, I'm really sorry."

Beth groped in her purse for a tissue. "It's horrible living in my house. We're all so scared, and I'm trying to keep it all together. I cut school three days last week just to get housework done and take care of Mom."

"What about your dad?"

A tear trickled from the corner of Beth's eye. "Dad left."

Erin stared, openmouthed. "Left?"

"He said he couldn't take the pressure anymore, and he packed up his things and took off about a month ago."

"Maybe he'll be back—"

"I don't think so. He hasn't even called to check on us. Not once in four weeks. My parents haven't gotten along for a while, you know. I guess this was just too much for Dad to handle."

Beth's situation made Erin feel as if lead weights had been hung on her heart. "Isn't there someone you could tell?"

"What am I supposed to tell? That I can't hack it? Do you know what Social Services does when it thinks kids are being neglected?"

"Social Services?"

"You know. The department for child welfare."

Erin nodded, pretending she understood. She only knew about welfare and such things through newspaper articles and TV news stories. Suddenly she wished she'd paid more attention to them. "What do they do?"

"They can come in and take us away from Mom and put us in foster homes, that's what. That would kill my mom. And it would be all my fault because I couldn't keep things together."

"But that's not fair. It's not your fault."

Beth slumped in her chair. "I'm thinking of dropping out of school."

"But you're only got a few months left till you graduate!"

"I'm barely scraping by now. My grades stink,

and they're not going to get any better until my mom's well. At least if I drop out and stay home, I'll be there for my brother and sisters."

"But there must be some other way. What does your mom say?"

"Oh, Erin, she's much too sick to even realize what's going on. She goes for dialysis every other day again—I can't dump this on her!"

"You gotta tell someone, Beth."

"I'm telling you."

"But I can't do anything to help."

"That's not true. Just telling you about it has made me feel better. I swear, I thought I was going to explode if I didn't get it out."

Erin wasn't sure she wanted Beth's burden. Beth might feel better now, but Erin was suddenly down in the pits. "I—I still think you should talk to somebody who can help you figure out what to do." For a moment Erin considered telling Beth about her own therapy, but she lacked the courage.

"I'll be okay," Beth said. She grasped Erin's arm. "You won't blab about this will you? You won't tell anyone and get me in trouble?"

"I don't have anybody to tell." She surprised herself with her confession. There was a time that she might have taken it to her parents, but now with so much tension in her own house, she couldn't talk to them anymore. She felt helpless. "How much time have you got before you have to be home?" she asked.

"An hour, tops."

Erin hauled Beth to her feet. "Then let's make the most of it. We'll do some shopping."

"Oh, I can't." Beth avoided Erin's eyes, making Erin realize that she probably didn't have any money for shopping.

"Um—I'm going to our spring dance—it's sort of like a prom—and I haven't had a chance to go shopping for a dress yet. Maybe you could help me pick something out."

Beth gave her a grateful look. "I really don't want to go home yet. Mom's resting, and I don't have to start supper for an hour. It would be fun to look at prom dresses—even though I won't be going to one."

In the department store Erin tried on several styles of dresses, and before long even she was caught up in the fun, despite her little white lie. She certainly hadn't decided to go to Spring Fling. Still, Beth seemed lost in the fantasy, and Erin was glad to help her forget her problems for even a little while.

Erin honestly hadn't meant to buy anything, but when she tried on a strapless dress in ice blue, Beth exclaimed, "That's gorgeous!"

The dress set off her eyes and ivory complexion like nothing else she'd owned. Before she knew it, Erin had bought it. "The guy you're going with will drool when he sees you in it," Beth said as they left the store.

The guy she was going with was the Invisible Man, Erin thought. "I really appreciate your helping me find something."

"It was fun for me too. I wish I . . ." her sentence trailed. "I'm glad I called you, Erin. Thanks for listening to me."

"I want you to keep calling me. Anytime. Please."

Beth agreed. "Just remember your promise to keep it a secret."

"I won't say a word. Don't forget, my play's next month. Please try to come."

Beth left, and Erin stood in the mall while people surged around her. Someone bumped her, and she spun, feeling like a leaf in a current of water with no control.

"What do you mean you bought a prom dress?" Shara stood in the center of the theater's dressing room with her hands on her hips. "I thought we were going shopping together."

Erin hadn't meant to upset Shara. She simply mentioned the dress in the course of conversation, hoping to brighten the mood after the rotten rehearsal they'd just had.

"And besides, when did you decide to go to the dance? When we talked the other day, you acted like it was the drudgery of the year."

"Shara, don't make such a big deal about it. Beth called me—you remember her—anyway, she was down in the dumps, so we met at the mall and started shopping just for fun."

"But you *know* how much I wanted to shop for dresses with you. Geez, Erin, that was a lousy thing to do."

"I bought a dress, Shara. It's not a federal offense, you know."

"Well excuse me for feeling like a reject!" Shara picked up her things and breezed out of the room.

"Terrific," Erin muttered, and chased after her. In the narrow hall she collided with David, who had already collided with Shara.

"What's the rush?" he asked.

"I have to go shopping for a dress," Shara said.

"Maybe I have one you could borrow," David said, grinning.

"I doubt it," Shara said. "We're not even the same size."

"I have a very nice wardrobe," David countered, tossing his arms around both their shoulders and tucking each under an arm. "You don't know what you're missing."

"I'll pass," Shara said.

"I already have a dress," Erin added, holding Shara's eyes with her own. "But I'm glad I ran into you because I do want to ask you something."

He bowed from the waist. "From your lips to heaven's ears."

"Briarwood's having a big dance, and Shara's asked Seth, and we thought it would be fun to double, so I'd like to know if you want to come with me." Her palms had gone clammy, and she could hardly believe what she was saying.

David blinked and then broke out into his dazzling smile. "Aw right!" Impulsively he caught her in a bear hug, lifting her off the ground.

"Save it for the dance numbers," Erin said, exasperated and flustered. Why did he have to act like such a kid?

Shara looked confused. "I'll call you later, Erin. I'm going to go tell Seth."

Alone with David, Erin felt timid. She hadn't meant to ask him; it had just happened. "I'll— um—get all the details to you tomorrow at rehearsal."

"Is this my day or what?"

"It's just a dance."

"But it's with you. A princess going with a frog."

Erin rolled her eyes. "Knock it off."

"You got a new dress?"

"Yes."

"What color?"

"Light blue."

David looked thoughtful. "I've got just the frock to match it," he said, and sauntered off.

A moment later his comment hit her. David Devlin was just crazy enough to show up in a dress, Erin thought. "David, wait! You're not going to embarrass me, are you?"

David turned innocent blue eyes on her. "You mean like wearing my clown makeup to the dance? Or is it something else you had in mind?"

"Let's just leave it for now," she told him. Wearing clown makeup to Spring Fling was something that Amy might have done. A terrible sense of melancholy stole over her as Beth's problems, the fight with Shara, and the memory of Amy bombarded her.

David caught his hand behind her neck and pulled her close. The teasing had gone out of his eyes. "I really want to go to the dance with you, Erin. Even clowns have their serious side."

That night her headache was the worst one she'd had in weeks. The medication didn't help, and it was nearly dawn before she fell into an exhausted sleep. Erin was in a stupor when her alarm sounded, so she told her mother to let her sleep in till noon, then she'd go to her afternoon classes.

The sunlight was streaming in her bedroom window when Mrs. Bennett barged in and shook Erin's shoulder. "Wake up, Erin. You have some explaining to do."

Erin opened her eyes and tried to focus. All she saw was her mother's grieved, tearful expression. "What's wrong?" Erin sat up slowly.

"Dr. Richardson just called. She said you've missed your last two appointments. What's going on? Why have you been lying to me?"

Chapter Ten

~~~

Swamped with guilt, Erin pulled the covers tighter as if to hide from her mother's wounded expression. "I didn't lie."

"You *said* you were going to therapy, then didn't go. What do you call it?"

"I got tied up with play practice and schoolwork and all. I just missed a couple of times."

"But you *must* understand the importance of this therapy in solving the mystery of your headaches," Mrs. Bennett admonished, twisting a wadded tissue as she spoke. "I want you to be well again, Erin. I couldn't stand it if something happened to you too."

By now Erin was starting to get angry—she hated the guilt trips her mother kept sending her on. She tossed off the covers and jumped to her feet, but the medication made her woozy, and she swayed.

Her mother reached out to steady her. "Just look at you—you're so groggy you can hardly stand up. Don't you realize that therapy is your only hope for getting rid of your headaches forever?"

"And don't you realize that sitting in that office

all by myself and having somebody dig around inside my head stinks?"

"Of course it's tough, honey. But you have so much ahead of you—college, career, family—everything. Why, someday you'll have kids of your own, and then you'll understand how I feel."

Kids of her own. She was the last of the Bennett line, because her father had no brothers or sisters. "Being married and having kids doesn't sound like such a hot idea to me."

"Why do you say that?"

Erin wanted to shout, "*Because yelling and fighting and leaving isn't fair.*" Instead she walked past her mother and started getting clothes together for school. "I need to get dressed."

Her mother took her arm. "Erin, please promise me you'll go back to Dr. Richardson this Thursday."

Her face looked pinched, and her tone sounded so pleading that Erin felt fresh waves of guilt. "Okay, I'll go."

"I'm counting on you to keep your promise." Mrs. Bennett sounded relieved.

"I'm your 'responsible' daughter. . . . Isn't that what you always used to tell me?"

"You still are."

Her mother stroked Erin's hair, and yet it was as if a great gulf separated them, and Erin didn't know how to get across. "Then I can't let you down, can I?"

"It's for your own sake," her mother called as Erin hurried toward the bathroom.

Erin shut the door and leaned against the wall,

fighting tears and feeling as if the weight of the world were on her shoulders. She turned on the faucets, and after the bathroom had filled with steam, she breathed deeply to relax and try to ward off a recurrence of her headache. The breathing exercises worked, and soon she felt better. Before climbing into the shower, she took her finger and wrote in the steam on the mirror: "Amy doesn't live here anymore." Then she smeared the words away and quickly showered and dressed.

Dr. Richardson treated her as if she'd never missed an appointment. Erin was relieved, because she couldn't have stood another lecture. The counselor's office seemed comfortable and homey, with framed passages of needlepoint on several of the walls. Curious, Erin thought, that she'd never noticed them before. She pointed at one. "Where'd you get these?"

"I do them. They relax me." It had never occurred to Erin that the therapist might have a life outside of her office. "What do you do to relax?" Dr. Richardson asked.

"I dance. The physical exercise makes me feel good."

"I tried aerobics once," Dr. Richardson said, "but there was nothing relaxing about grunting and sweating." She wrinkled her nose to make her point.

Erin giggled, glad that they weren't probing into her mind right away. She studied the intricate scrollwork of one particular needlepoint and read aloud, "'Is there no Balm in Gilead; is there no physician there?' What's that mean?"

"Gilead was a place in the Middle East where a legendary balm with miraculous healing powers was supposed to have come from. You simply smoothed it on, and all your diseases disappeared. Caravans used to bring it out of Gilead to sell to the rest of the known world."

"Too bad you can't find some of it and rub it into my head."

Dr. Richardson tapped her desk with a pencil. "For me the balm of Gilead is what I try to apply to people's hearts and souls, because healing begins from the inside out."

"Do you think I'll ever get well?"

"The fact that you're here, trying, encourages me."

"But just talking doesn't seem to be doing much."

"Aren't there longer and longer gaps between your headaches?"

"Yes, but I still can't figure out what's triggering them. I've been fine for a while, then the other day I was just talking to David, and bang—one hit me hard."

"How are you and David getting along?"

"Better." Erin felt her cheeks color. "I asked him to our school's formal dance."

"I'd say you were doing better. What changed your mind about him?"

Erin laced her fingers together in her lap. "We

talked. I went with him to see his clown routine, and I met his kid sister. She's deaf."

"But there's still something about him that sort of gets under your skin, huh?"

Dr. Richardson's perception amazed Erin. "It's like he *likes* being different, as if he goes out of his way to be outrageous."

"And that seems to bother you."

Erin stared at the carpet for a moment, trying to put her thoughts into words. "In the beginning he actually brought on some of my headaches, but now, in some weird way, he helps keep them away. I can't figure out why."

Dr. Richardson didn't say anything right away. When she did speak, her question seemed off the topic. "Erin, tell me what your sister Amy was like."

Startled, Erin looked up. "Cute. Everybody liked her, but she had some pretty annoying habits. She was *never* on time, and she could talk me into doing anything for her—which used to make me really mad. But I couldn't help myself. She'd always rope me into doing whatever she wanted. She was never serious about anything, except wanting to be a great actress. Like the world was waiting for Amy to make an appearance. She didn't take life very seriously. But then David says I take life *too* serious—" She stopped talking as insight swept over her.

"You look surprised. Tell me what you're thinking."

"It's Amy and David. They're a lot alike, you know? I—I never realized that until now."

"How does that make you feel?"

Erin wasn't sure. "Strange, that's all. Gee, I don't see how the world could handle *two* Amys."

"But David's David."

"Yes, that's true. They're different, but they're alike too. He does silly, goofy things like Amy would. We had a slime fight after rehearsal one day. When Amy was in the eighth grade, she led a Jell-O war in the school cafeteria."

"Does it make you feel sad to remember?"

"No," Erin said slowly. "But it makes me want to see her and talk to her again."

"If you could see and talk to her, what would you share?"

Erin shook her head. "I don't know. And I don't feel like talking about it right now."

"There are several kids your age in my support group who've lost a sister or brother."

Lost. The therapist made it sound as if the person could be found. As if death wasn't final and irrevocable. Erin thought of Beth, who might be "losing" her mother.

"Will you think about coming? We'd love to have you."

"Maybe. Look, I've got to get back to school for evening play practice. My dad's got a meeting at school tonight too, and his car's in the shop, so I have to give him a ride home." Erin knew she was making an excuse to bow out of the session early but didn't care. She wanted to leave.

Dr. Richardson walked her to the office door, where Erin turned and gestured toward the framed needlepoint about Gilead. "If any caravans pass through selling that stuff, buy some for me."

Dr. Richardson asked, "Do you know what 'debridement' is, Erin?" She shook her head. "When a person's been badly burned, the dead skin has to be removed, or debrided. The skin is literally scrubbed off the wounds."

Erin grimaced. "That must hurt."

"It's very painful, but unless it's done, the burn victim can't begin to heal."

"So what's that got to do with me?"

"There's something inside you—something about your sister's death—that's trying to get out. Your headaches are an expression of that 'something.' These sessions with me, and meeting with the support group, is a kind of debridement for your psyche. No matter how much it hurts, it has to be done so that you can be all right again."

"So there is no magic balm?" Erin asked wistfully.

"Only in the figurative sense. And you can't buy it either, you have to seek it on your own."

Erin sighed and left, unsure if she had the strength for the hunt.

The play rehearsal went so smoothly that Ms. Thornton and Mr. Ault let everybody go home early. Not wanting to linger afterward, Erin quickly gathered her things and hurried to her father's classroom. She approached the room cautiously, unable to forget the day she'd stopped by the school and discovered him weeping. She'd never told him, but the memory of his tears haunted her still.

Erin stopped at the closed door, listened, then knocked.

"Come in," Mr. Bennett said. Erin entered to see him putting papers into his briefcase. "Hi," he said, and smiled. "I thought I'd be the one waiting on you."

"We got out early. Are you finished?"

"I sent the Lowerys home with their promise to make Pam work harder in my class. She's bright enough, but she just doesn't apply herself. She's not nearly the student your teachers tell me you are, Erin."

She shrugged. "That's me . . . little Miss Einstein."

"Don't make light of it. I know it must be tough putting in time for that play and still keeping up with your schoolwork."

They walked to Erin's car and got in. The night had turned cool, and the smell of rain was in the air. She turned on the engine. In the glow of the mercury lamppost, the outside world looked colorless.

Her father asked, "Say, I've got an idea. How'd you like your old man to treat you to a hot fudge sundae?"

Surprised, Erin asked, "But we've got school tomorrow, and it's already after ten." Big drops of rain splattered against the windshield. She turned on the wipers.

"Oh, come on. It'll be like old times. Just you

and me and Amy and—" His voice stopped, and Erin's heart squeezed. Rain pummeled the car. The headlights cut a sweeping arc through the darkness, and Amy's ghost wedged between them in the seat.

Chapter Eleven

❧

Erin was the first to recover. "I think a hot fudge sundae sounds yummy," she said with an enthusiasm she didn't feel.

"Me too," Mr. Bennett said quietly.

Erin drove cautiously, because the rain made the road slick. At the minimall she parked, and they ran for cover into the old-fashioned ice cream parlor, where waiters were dressed in white shirts and red-striped vests.

Once in a booth, Erin asked, "Are you gonna call Mom?"

"She said she'd be going to bed early, so I don't think she'll miss us." Mr. Bennett didn't meet Erin's eyes as he spoke.

They ordered, and once the waiter had gone, Mr. Bennett asked, "Do you want to talk about what happened in the car?"

"What happened?"

"When I said Amy's name. I didn't mean to, but for a moment I forgot she wasn't with us."

Erin felt panic, because she was certain she saw a mist cover his eyes. "That's all right," she said quickly. "Dr. Richardson says it's good to talk about her."

"How's it going with the counselor?"

"She says I'm making progress."

"She wanted us to come in as a family at first."

The news surprised Erin. "So why didn't we?"

"Your mother felt it wasn't necessary. You were the one with the headaches."

Erin wasn't surprised by this information, but it still annoyed her. Why did her parents act as if *she* was the only one with a problem? Couldn't they see how they were growing apart? "I'm really trying hard to get well, Dad. Honest."

"I know, and I'm not sure it's something you should be going through by yourself."

Their ice cream arrived, and Erin ate a spoonful of whipped cream, but it was too sweet, and the taste clung to her mouth. "Dr. Richardson thinks that I'm not over Amy's death."

"Who is?" he asked heavily.

"It's been over a year," Erin said.

"Is there a time limit on these things?"

"I guess not. I miss Amy too." For a moment Erin's voice sounded thick. She wanted to tell him, *"But Daddy, I'm still here."* Instead, she asked, "I guess no one can ever take Amy's place, huh?"

Mr. Bennett shoved his sundae aside. "You and Amy were always so different from one another. Maybe it was because you were the firstborn, and your mother and I wanted so many things for you. Parents go a little overboard for the firstborn, you know."

"You didn't expect things of Amy?"

"We did, but it was different."

Erin wanted to say, "*You bet it was different. You always let Amy do anything she wanted.*" Instead, she said, "Amy used to wonder why she was short and dark-haired and I was tall and blond."

"You take after my great-grandmother, Emily Eckloe."

"I do?"

"Yes. Amy resembled your mother's side of the family—small and dark. But Emily was from Norway, and a real beauty. I think she studied classical ballet but gave up her career to marry great-granddad."

So *she* was the oddball of the family, not Amy. For some reason the information pleased her. "That sounds romantic, but I can't imagine giving up my dancing."

"Not even for love?"

Erin blushed. "Especially for love."

"I guess that love doesn't have much to recommend to you."

She knew he was alluding to his own crumbling relationship. "It's okay for other people, but I've got lots of other things I want to do first. Books and movies make it seem sort of corny, like it's nothing but butterflies in your stomach."

"That's where it usually starts, and there's no substitute for it in the world. Don't tell me you've never gone through the butterfly stage."

She thought of how simply seeing Travis used to make her feel gooey inside. "I guess I have, but I knew it wasn't the real thing."

"That's supposed to be my line," Mr. Bennett joked. "How did you come to that conclusion?"

"Probably because I was always so busy with my dancing. It's always seemed more important than guys and dating."

"I understand that. Love starts out with such enthusiasm, but somehow it gets lost between mortgage payments and kids in the right schools and jobs that pay enough money. . . ." He rubbed his eyes. "I sound cynical, don't I?"

"Just tired." He seemed defeated. "Would you rather have a job someplace besides Briarwood?"

There was a long pause between her question and his answer. "Do you know what I really wanted to be when I was in college?" Erin shrugged. "A novelist," he told her.

"A writer?"

"Not just *any* writer. I wanted to live in the East Village in New York, or maybe even Paris, and write 'meaningful' books about life and the universe."

"Why didn't you?"

Mr. Bennett gave her a poignant smile. "It wasn't very practical. Besides, I met your mother, we married, and then you came along, so starving in the Village became less appealing. I guess that's why I encouraged you and Amy when you took to dancing and acting."

Thinking back, Erin realized that it had always been her father who had favored her dance lessons and encouraged Amy's acting skills. Why hadn't she seen that before? "Remember how you used to read to us when we were little?" she asked.

"And Amy would ask a million questions about why Humpty Dumpty fell off the wall—" he said.

"And why couldn't they put him back together again."

"You used to get so exasperated, you'd clamp your hand over her mouth."

"I read that old book to her when she was in the hospital," Erin confessed, sheepishly. "I knew she couldn't hear me, because they said she was brain dead, but I read it anyway."

Her father studied her, then said, "Oh yeah? So did I."

"You did?" Goose bumps broke out on her arms. "The nurses must have thought we were crazy."

"She was my little princess."

Erin felt a surge of envy. Hadn't she always felt that Amy was 'Daddy's little girl,' and that she was just the 'responsible one'?

"Are you sorry?" she asked. "Do you wish you could do it all again and go off and write novels instead of being a teacher?"

"No. You can't trade what is for what might have been. Besides, if I had, I would never have had you or Amy, would I?"

"Sure you would have, but we would have been born in Paris."

He took her hand. "No. You would not have been born at all."

She tried to imagine nonexistence but

couldn't. "I'll go to Paris for you," she said. "I'll dance and be the hit of Europe."

"Not for me, Erin. For *you*." *And for Amy*, she thought, because her sister would never be able to realize her dreams either.

Her father reached over and clasped her hand. "And don't be so down on falling in love. Love can be very good."

"Not to worry," she said, faking enthusiasm. "I'll be on the lookout for Mr. Right." Yet she knew deep down that falling in love was the last thing she wanted to do. "Dad," she asked, choosing her words carefully. "Do you ever feel like leaving?"

"Leaving? Where would I go?"

"Off to Paris to write novels?" She said it with a smile, but her heart was hammering.

"Those were silly dreams, long ago. No, I won't go away."

She wanted desperately to believe him, because she didn't think she could stand to lose her father too. "I'll be going away in the fall," she ventured.

"You want to very much, don't you?"

She nodded vigorously. "But you and Mom seem against it. Mom more so than you."

"Letting go is hard, that's all."

"But I *have* to go. I just want . . ." Words failed her. She wanted so much to be a good daughter, but she also wanted to live her own life. "Well, you know," she finished lamely.

He picked up the check. "You want to be out on your own. It's natural. I guess we should discuss it with Dr. Richardson. I'll—uh—talk to your mother about it."

They drove home in silence, with Erin feeling detached. She was glad she'd talked to her father. It had helped for her to see him as an individual. He'd had dreams and plans for his life too, but they got changed as surely as Amy's had. Later that night she lay in her bed and wondered what kind of books he would have written. Through the darkness she heard muffled, but loud, words. Erin couldn't make them out, but she recognized their angry tone. Later she heard a door slam, and she rolled over and stared at the wall, knowing that her father had gone down the hall to sleep in another room.

"Are you *really* going to eat that?" Erin asked David the next afternoon at the mall as the clerk in the ice cream store handed him a cone heaped with three different flavors.

"Every bite," David said, taking a mouthful from the top.

Jody pulled on his arm and signed him a message. Erin watched as David signed a reply. "My sister wants the same thing," he told Erin.

"Make mine vanilla, and only one scoop," Erin insisted.

"Boring," David said, but placed the order anyway.

Erin observed David and Jody covertly, still wondering how she'd let him talk her into coming to the mall when he'd appeared on her doorstep that Saturday afternoon, uninvited. She supposed it was his little-boy charm. And his sister. Erin found the little girl adorable. Her big blue green eyes, curly blond hair, and infectious smile—so like David's—were hard to resist. Erin was also intrigued by the child's deafness. She'd never known a handicapped person, and the way Jody adapted to the regular world fascinated her.

After they'd sat down, Erin said, "Jody doesn't miss much, does she?"

"She's got a very high IQ. Once she figured out signing and broke through the communications barrier, she was off like a shot."

Jody signed something to Erin. "I don't understand," Erin told David.

"You should learn to sign," David said. "Then you can talk to Jody yourself."

"Oh, I could never learn—"

"Sure you can! It's easy. Watch." He made slow, deliberate moves with his hands and fingers.

"That's Jody's name, isn't it?"

"Very good. You remembered. Now here's yours, and here's mine." She watched, then mimicked his movements. "You're a natural," David said.

"But it doesn't seem like you spell out every word when you talk to Jody. I mean, that would take forever."

"That's the beauty of signing. Certain gestures stand for nouns and even complete phrases. For instance . . ." David drew his thumb along his cheek and down his jawbone. "This means 'girl.'" He repeated the movement, adding a circular motion with his open palm in front of his face. "That means pretty girl."

Jody tugged on Erin's arm, made similar gestures, and added the letters of Erin's name. "What do you guess she's just said to you?" David asked.

"I think she just told me that *I* was a pretty girl."

"You got it!" David smiled, and Erin dropped her eyes because it made her quivery inside. "Now try this," David said. He held up his hand and tucked his two middle fingers against his palm so that only his thumb, forefinger and pinky were extended.

"I give up," Erin said.

He repeated the move while saying the words, "I love you."

His aqua-colored eyes were so bright that they seemed to glow. Erin's stomach did a somersault, and she felt a tightness in her chest, as if her breath couldn't find a way out. She jumped to her feet. "I'm going to get a drink of water. I saw a fountain near the entrance of the food court."

"Hurry back," David called. "There's lots to learn."

She didn't want to learn anymore. David made her feel things she hadn't felt in over a year. She didn't want to care about David Devlin. She really didn't.

"Erin!" Someone called her name, and she spun.

A tall boy with black hair and chocolate-colored eyes was coming toward her through the crowd. For a heart-stopping moment Erin stared as Travis Sinclair walked her way.

Chapter Twelve

For Erin time stood still, and she saw Travis, not in the mall, but in the moonlight on the sidewalk that surrounded Tampa Bay. She could almost hear the lapping water and smell the jasmine-scented night air.

Travis approached her tentatively, his thumbs hooked on the belt loops of his jeans. "Hi," he said. "I was just coming in the door, and I thought I recognized you, so I hollered."

Erin felt her mouth settle into a grim line. "I thought you were away at college."

"It's spring break. My roommates and I are down for the week. You know, the beach and all."

She remembered last year at spring break she was supposed to go to the beach with Shara and some friends and flirt with the college guys. But Amy had been hooked to life support. "Have you seen Cindy?" She arched the words, like barbs.

Travis reddened and shifted from foot to foot. "I told you once before, Cindy's nothing to me. I never went out with her again after the dance."

Erin was angry. She wanted to hurt him; she wanted to run away. "Well, I'd like to say it was good to see you again, Travis, but why lie?"

"I was hoping you weren't still mad at me, Erin. I was hoping that you might have figured out how hard it was for me to see Amy that way—"

"Save it!" She might have said more, but David appeared and stepped between her and Travis.

"I'm David Devlin," he said. "Weren't you a senior last year at Berkshire?"

Travis nodded at David. "Yeah. I remember you. How is the old place? Is Mr. Wells still there?"

"Yep. He'll never retire. I think we're gonna cast him in bronze and set him out for the pigeons."

Erin listened while David and Travis traded school memories, and when Travis turned to leave, she refused to say good-bye. "What was that all about?" he asked.

"I don't know what you mean."

"I looked out and saw the two of you standing in the middle of the food court, and it looked like you were arguing. So don't pretend nothing was going on."

"It's not important."

He took her arm and pulled her closer. "I want to know what's between you and Travis Sinclair. Were you seeing him? I know he had plenty of girlfriends."

"Hardly," Erin said. "I hate his guts." David looked surprised. "What's wrong?" she asked. "Is it so hard to believe that every girl doesn't fall at his feet?" She played up the sarcasm because she knew deep down how much she had once cared about him, and she didn't want anyone *ever* to know.

She'd told Amy, but the truth had been buried with her.

"*Talk* to me. Tell me what's wrong."

Erin felt a tightness in her head as if a band had been clamped around it. "I need to go home. Where's Jody?"

David let go of her arm and stared at her hard. "Jody's waiting in the ice cream shop."

She felt sorry for him suddenly. David hadn't done anything wrong, and neither had Jody. They both must think she had flipped, but there was too much to tell, too much she didn't want to tell. "David, I'm not trying to hide anything from you. It's just that I'm getting this little headache, and if it gets out of control . . ."

"You do look sort of pale."

They left the mall, and Erin rested her head against the back of the seat during the drive home. By the time they arrived, she was almost blind from the pain. Her parents weren't there, so David took her to her room while Jody waited in the living room. He pulled back the covers, and she slid beneath the sheets, fully clothed. "I don't want to leave you," he said.

"Go. Please." Erin's voice was barely a whisper. She was afraid she was going to throw up, and she didn't want him to see that.

He tucked the covers around her chin and touched her cheek. "I'm gonna call and check on you later."

"Much later," she told him and groaned. After he'd gone and she was alone, Erin began to cry. The tears trickled down, and inexplicably they washed away some of the pain. "No need to wonder what set this one into motion, Dr. Richardson," Erin said aloud as if the shadows in her room would answer. Seeing Travis had triggered this headache. But knowing the cause didn't mean a cure. She longed to go to Gilead and find some magic balm. Instead, she cried herself to sleep.

"I thought you gave up cigarettes, Mom." Mrs. Bennett's back was to Erin, but she could see the thin trail of blue smoke curling upward from where her mother was sitting in the office she'd converted from Amy's old bedroom. The computer terminal on her desk blinked amber with a spreadsheet.

Mrs. Bennett stabbed out the cigarette and spun toward the doorway. "Don't sneak up on me, Erin. And I only smoke when I'm under a lot of stress. Summer's not even here, and already I've got to start buying for the store's fall line. Where have you been all afternoon anyway?"

"Tonight's Spring Fling, remember? Shara and I went to have our nails done." She held them out for her mother's inspection.

"Well, come closer. I can't see them from here."

Erin hesitated, then walked across the sun-filled room. It still made her uncomfortable, even though it looked nothing like Amy's old room. Bookshelves stood in the place of Amy's dresser, and her mother's desk took up the space where the bed once stood. The walls had been repainted a soft yellow, and the red gingham curtains replaced with decorative wooden blinds. At least the beige-colored carpet was the same. "I think the pink will go well with the blue of my dress, don't you?"

Mrs. Bennett inspected Erin's hands. "Yes, but I still wish you'd picked out your dress from stock at the boutique. You would have only paid cost for it."

"Don't you like my dress?"

"It's pretty, but it was so expensive."

Erin held her tongue and sauntered over to the bookshelves. Instead of Amy's collection of teen romances, Erin studied the bindings of books on computer software, accounting, and fashion. "Did you always want to do this, Mom? Be in fashion and own your own business?"

Mrs. Bennett leaned back in her swivel chair. "I was always interested in clothes, but I bought the store with the money your grandmother left me in her will. You and Amy were growing up, and I needed to work so that we could afford to send you both to college. It seemed like a good investment at the time."

Just one to send now, Erin thought. "Florida State shouldn't be too expensive," she said, half holding her breath because the topic usually brought on a negative comment from her mother. "I mean with in-state tuition and all. Then what will you do with the money? Dad told me he once wanted to travel—to Paris."

"Paris." Mrs. Bennett laughed. "Isn't that typical of him? I've always been the more practical of the two of us. I'll save the money, of course. It takes years of hard work to build up a nest egg. I don't imagine you'll want to take care of us in our old age."

Erin hadn't ever thought about it. When she was nine, her grandmother had lived with them until she died. She figured that she and Amy would simply help each other out with family problems after they grew up. "I'd work it out. Taking care of you and Daddy, that is."

"If my business continues to do well, you won't have to."

In other words, Erin thought, she wouldn't be needed. She wondered if her mother would still need her father if her business continued to grow. Erin retreated to the farthest corner of the room. A desktop copier stood on a short file cabinet. Once Amy's vanity table had lined the wall, and a poster of Tom Cruise had hung to one side. "I guess I should start getting ready. I wanted to take a long bath this afternoon."

"Just a minute," Mrs. Bennett said. "Have you written down exactly where you'll be tonight like I asked you to?"

Erin counted to ten under her breath. "Yes. The Columbia restaurant, the dance at the downtown Hilton, and then to Shara's parents' beach house."

"David *is* a good driver, isn't he? I wish I'd met his family. And absolutely no alcohol. Is that clear?"

"Don't you trust me?"

"I *know* what prom night is all about, Erin. Kids can get into a lot of trouble."

"Well, I'm not like other kids. I didn't even want to go at first, but Shara talked me into it."

"I'm just concerned about you. It's not like there'll be another prom night around here, you know."

Erin dropped her gaze to the carpet. A round, colorless spot stared up at her. She remembered the time when Amy had spilled nail polish and tried to take it off with acetone and had removed the color from the carpet instead. "Why are you always griping at me?" she asked her mother.

"That's ridiculous. I just want you to be extra careful tonight. You never used to care if I reminded you of things. Why can't it be like it used to between us?"

"Nothing's the same anymore." Erin's palms began to sweat.

"Are you saying that it's my fault things are different? I've done all I can to keep the lines of communication open between us."

Erin felt that Jody was better at communicating than her mother. "I need to start getting ready," she said, and started toward the doorway.

"You're all I have, Erin," her mother blurted. "I can't help but worry about you. In time I know you'll go away, and then . . ." Her sentence trailed, and Erin saw tears fill her eyes.

She wanted to cry too. "You've still got Daddy," she ventured.

Her mother looked away. "And he wants to go to Paris."

They'd come full circle in their argument, and

for an instant Erin felt as if she were on a merry-go-round. "I'll be in my room getting ready," she said. "David's supposed to be here at six, and then we're picking up Seth and Shara."

"I'll make sure there's film in the camera."

She felt like asking, "What for?" Mrs. Bennett no longer kept up the photo albums. The prints of Amy's sixteenth birthday were still in a drawer. At the doorway Erin paused. "Oh, David's sort of unconventional, so there's no telling what he'll show up wearing."

"Yes, I remember the time he came here in his clown outfit. I hope he uses better sense tonight." Her mother swiveled toward the desk and her computer terminal. "I'll be here if you need any help getting ready."

Erin realized that she couldn't begin to tell her mother what she needed from her. "What's Dad doing this afternoon?"

Mrs. Bennett shrugged. "He's at the library, I think. Safe and sound in his world of books," she added under her breath.

"Maybe he'll write one someday," Erin said.

"Don't bank on it. He talks a lot but does very little."

Erin wanted to say something to defend him but didn't know what. Wistfully she watched her mother begin to type on the computer keyboard and tune Erin out, as if she'd already left the room. Sunlight fell across her mother's shoulders and caught in her hair, which was dark, like Amy's.

Chapter Thirteen

~

Erin fidgeted with her hair and looked at her alarm-clock radio for the umpteenth time. She'd been ready for half an hour, and she still had time to kill before David was due to arrive. Her parents were waiting in the living room; she heard the TV playing, yet she knew that her father was reading and her mother was compiling lists of new designs and fabrics for the store. She wished they would talk to each other, like they used to do. Erin sighed, not wanting the tension in her home to spoil the excitement she felt about the night ahead of her.

She rechecked her evening bag for all the essentials, including her headache medicine. Her stomach growled, reminding her that she'd skipped dinner in anticipation of the meal at the Columbia. She went to her dresser, to the drawer where she kept an emergency cache of candy bars, and poked through her lingerie and dance leotards. At the back of the drawer, she felt a piece of paper caught between the side and a groove, buried under stuff she hadn't worn in ages. She jiggled the drawer and pulled out the paper. It was the program from the night she'd gone to a rock concert with Travis. He was supposed to take Amy, but when Amy was grounded for not finishing a history paper on time, she begged Erin to go in her place so Travis wouldn't take Cindy Pitzer. Erin opened the program. Inside was scrawled,

> *Surprise, sis! Hope this doesn't ruin your souvenir, but I couldn't pass up the temptation to sign an autograph. Someday this will be a program with MY name on it!*

> *Love and stuff,*

> *Your tragic Russian princess from the night of her term paper on the Crimean War—aka AMY!*

Erin remembered the night as if it had been last week. It had been a washout, because all Travis talked about was Amy, and Erin finally understood how hopeless her crush was. Later, on that last night with Amy in the hospital, Erin had confessed to her sister: "And I've decided that it wasn't that I really loved *Travis*. I just wanted somebody to love and somebody who loved me the way it is in the books and movies."

Well, she didn't want that anymore. In real life, people who swore to "love, honor, and cherish" each other turned into strangers who argued and shouted and spent more time apart than together. In the real world daddies went away and didn't call home. So much for commitment.

Erin traced her finger over Amy's hastily scribbled words, imagining her sister sneaking the program into the drawer as a special surprise. *Amy should be here tonight,* Erin thought. They should be getting ready together. Amy would be clowning around, and Erin would be trying to keep a straight face and ignore her antics. And then their dates would come, and Amy would do something outrageous, like pin her corsage to her hair and—

"Erin, David's here." Erin jumped at the sound of her mother's voice.

"Coming," she said, stuffing the program into the drawer.

In the hall her mother said, "If you weren't going with Shara, I'd never let you go out with this boy, Erin."

"What's the matter?"

"See for yourself."

Erin hurried into the living room. David stood facing her father but turned and flashed his high-voltage grin. He was wearing a tuxedo jacket, ruffled white shirt, paisley blue cummerbund and bow tie, and faded jeans. Down the side seams he'd sewn a blue satin ribbon. He wore red high-top sneakers and a black top hat, and a vivid red scarf poked from the upper outside pocket of his jacket. His bright red clown nose covered his real one.

Erin felt embarrassed. Couldn't David take something seriously, just once? He hastily tugged off the false nose. "Just kidding about the nose," he told her, and held out the plastic box with her corsage.

Inside lay an exquisite cluster of violets and miniature orchids. "Do they squirt water?" she asked sarcastically.

"I'm a clown, not an idiot," he said.

"Why don't I get a few photos?" Mr. Bennett said, eyeing David skeptically. For a moment Erin was afraid her mother would remind him to please drive carefully, but somehow they made it out the door without her mother hovering too much and her father asking too many dumb questions.

Outside, the moon glowed full and bright. David took her arm and turned her toward him. "You really do look beautiful," he said. "I wish I had a real coach to take you in."

Still peeved, Erin said, "Thanks." She was half-afraid to see the car he was driving, but when she looked, it was a standard station wagon.

David inserted a cassette into the tape deck and began to talk as they drove to pick up Seth and Shara at Shara's house. Erin made appropriate but nominal answers, all the while thinking how long it had been since she'd been out on a date. Not that she hadn't been asked, but she hadn't accepted any since before Amy had died. For the life of her, she couldn't recall why she'd always said no. And now that she was finally going out, it was with a guy like David, who wasn't at all her type.

Shara and Seth climbed into the backseat, chattering and teasing David about his clothes, and when they walked into the restaurant, heads turned. Erin wished again that he hadn't dressed so weird.

After dinner they arrived at the Hilton, where a valet parked the car. The grand ballroom reminded Erin of something out of Hollywood, glitzy and shimmering with crystal chandeliers and pink-linen-draped tables decorated with floral and candlelight centerpieces. She recognized friends from Briarwood, waved and smiled gaily, all the while noticing how her classmates kept eyeing David.

"Let's dance," he said, and led her to an oak parquet floor where an ensemble band played soft rock music. Erin had danced with David a hundred times in play rehearsals, but this time it wasn't the same. "You're stiff," he told her. "Come closer. I won't bite."

"Is that a promise?"

David's expression seemed puzzled and hurt. "Erin, you're supposed to be having fun."

"I am."

"How can you tell?"

Around them couples clung together, silk and taffeta rustling as they moved. Erin wanted to be like them. More than anything she wanted to be a part of the tradition of prom night. "Maybe we should sit this one out," she told David.

He caught her hand. "Maybe you should tell me what's bothering you." She said nothing. "You don't like my tux?" She felt her cheeks redden and felt petty. "This is *me*, Erin," David said earnestly. "I'm not ever going to be just like everybody else. I thought you understood that."

"Look at us, Erin," Amy said. "You're tall,

blond, and graceful and I'm—well, short, round, and fully packed."

"What's your point?"

"We're different, that's all. You got the looks, talent, and brains and I got—"

"Does it bother you?" David asked.

"What?"

"That I'm different from your idea of Mr. Wonderful."

"How do you know what I like or don't like?"

"I saw the way you looked at Travis Sinclair."

"I told you, I hate him."

Seth and Shara danced past. Seth leaned over and said, "You two sure have a strange way of dancing with each other. You're supposed to move like this—" He demonstrated by dipping Shara backward.

Erin was grateful for the interruption, but David said, "Buzz off, Seth."

"I can take a hint. But first, lend me your hanky. I'm dripping."

Perspiration stood out on Seth's forehead, and David reached in his outside top pocket for the red hanky and pulled. Seth took it, but it didn't stop coming. The four of them stood transfixed as the material kept sliding out of David's pocket. Around them other couples stopped dancing and closed ranks. Giggles started, then swelled into laughter, as the "hanky" looped and draped to the floor in an endless stream of multicolored cloth.

Determined, Seth kept pulling. "Trick hanky?" Seth asked with a bemused smile. Shara giggled.

"Gosh, you're quick," David told him.

"You're a real clown, Devlin."

The hanky finally pulled free, and David bowed politely from the waist. Around them, the crowd burst into applause. Erin kept wishing she could sink through the floor, unable to remember when she'd felt so embarrassed.

"Stop being such a show-off, Amy!"

"Gosh, Erin, I'm sorry. Am I embarrassing you?"

"I embarrassed you again, didn't I?" David stooped to pick up his handkerchief. The music had stopped, and couples were walking toward the tables. "I don't do it on purpose, you know. I mean, I really did want to bring this gag hanky along tonight, but I had no idea it would come out right in the middle of the dance floor."

"Let's just forget the whole thing, okay?"

"If you'll give me a smile."

Erin managed one.

"How about a kiss?"

"Don't push your luck."

Erin went to the ladies' room, where girls surrounded her. "Where did you find him?" someone asked. "He's hysterical."

"We're in the play together."

"He's adorable," another exclaimed.

"Do you think so?"

"Come on, Erin, you *know* he is."

"Yeah, better than the dud that I brought along," another girl said.

Erin toyed with tendrils of hair around her face. So the girls thought David was cool, a real find. She fumbled in her purse and dug out her headache pills and washed one down with water from the spigot. She was feeling all right, but she remembered the times David unwittingly *had* brought on a headache. *No need to take chances*, she told her reflection silently.

The evening passed, with David gathering people to him as flowers attracted honeybees. He dragged Erin to a flower-draped indoor trellis, where a photographer took a souvenir photo. And at midnight, when everyone began to leave, he stood near the door and issued "blessings" like the pope.

All the way to Shara's beach house, they laughed and joked, with Erin in the thick of the banter. Yet she felt as if she were divided into halves. Half of her acted gay and happy, while the other half seemed disengaged, like a spectator sitting on the sidelines.

At the beach house music blasted, and while David wormed his way into the kitchen for sodas, Erin slipped out the door and headed up the moonstruck beach. She welcomed the quiet and the salt air that filled her lungs and stung her eyes.

The water lapped against the shore, and moonlight flecked the caps of waves, reminding her, inexplicably, of Travis's eyes. *"I told you once that I'd*

*never met anybody like Amy. She was wild and a
little bit crazy, and we had a million laughs together. But when I walked into that hospital room,
when I saw her lying on that bed with tubes and
wires and hoses—"*

A seagull circled and called forlornly. Erin
started. She was accustomed to seeing gulls in the
daytime when they scoured the beach for food, but
here in the darkness the bird seemed out of place.

*Travis said, "See, Erin, your problem is that
everybody has to act exactly the same way for it to
be legitimate with you."*

The gull swooped lower, then hung in midair
until an updraft caught its wings and tossed it
higher. It flew away, its cry blending with the
sounds of the sea.

*"Let her go, Erin. For everybody's sake, let
Amy go."*

Erin felt moisture on her cheeks and wondered
how the salt spray could have splashed against her
face when there was hardly any breeze. Her knees
began to give way, and she sank into the warm,
gritty sand. She wrapped her arms around herself
and began to rock back and forth. The wetness on
her face tingled in the cool night air. Sobs began
deep inside her throat, little choking noises, desperate to get out.

Salt water splashed the front of her new blue
dress, but she didn't care. All she heard was the
drone of the sea that blurred with the memory of
hissing ventilators and beeping monitors. The
rhythmic litany whispered, "Alone . . . alone . . .
alone . . ."

Chapter Fourteen

~~~

"Erin, what's wrong?" David was suddenly beside her, on his knees in the sand. She shook her head, unable to speak. He pulled her up and hugged her to his chest. "It's all right," he said again and again.

She remembered the night at the pizza parlor when he'd held her while she cried. He must think her an awful baby. "I—I don't know what's the matter with me. I'm so mixed up."

"About what?"

"Sometimes I feel happy and on top of life, then other times I feel so sad. Like in the car, driving over here—wasn't I laughing and having fun?"

"It seemed like you were."

"I really *was*. And now . . . I just went out for a little walk and . . . and . . . all I want to do is cry." She pushed away from him but grabbed his lapels. "Maybe I'm going crazy. Do you think that could be it?"

"We all have our ups and downs."

She shook her head vehemently. "I hear voices too. Conversations that I had over a year ago. I'll be right in the middle of talking to somebody, and these memories come flooding into my mind. I tell you, I can *really* hear things."

"What things? Who's talking?"

"Amy, mostly." She was about to say, *Travis, too*, but decided against it. "And so many things remind me of her. A million things . . . everywhere I look."

David smoothed her hair, which had tumbled from its combs. "Come on," he urged, and led her behind a small sand berm that the wind had built up over time. He spread his jacket and sat her down on it. He sat beside her, raised his knees, and pulled her gently across his lap. "I don't think you're crazy," he said, rubbing her cheek with the back of his hand.

Erin responded as if she hadn't heard him. "But there are other times when I can't even remember what she looked like. How her face was shaped, or how her voice sounded. That seems to me like I'm going crazy." She kicked off her shoes and dug her stocking feet into the sand.

"Well, to me it seems like you're only trying to hold on to her. Life goes on, Erin. I know that sounds corny, but it's true. And what happens every day sort of shoves the past further away. It's natural."

"But I don't want to forget Amy. It's—it's disloyal."

"I don't think you'll ever forget her," David said, sifting sand through his fingers. "But you can't make a saint of her either."

For the first time Erin smiled. "Amy, a saint?

Not on a bet! Sometimes she was a real goof-up. She was always promising to do things for people—you know, help out. She meant to do them too, but she always promised more than she could deliver. I can't tell you how many times I had to bail her out, fill in for her at Mom's store and do her chores as well as mine. She could twist my parents around her little finger."

"Yeah, I know what you mean. Jody's that way. Whatever she wants, she gets. We all have to work real hard at not feeling sorry for her just because she's deaf."

The sand muffled the sound of the ocean and was making Erin feel warm and snuggly. "It used to make me mad," Erin confessed. "Amy got away with murder because she was the 'baby.'"

"Try being a guy who likes acting and clowning instead of law, like his father." David glanced away. "Sometimes my father treats me like I must have been switched at birth in the hospital."

Erin felt a jab of guilt. How little she knew about David! "Why do you suppose parents do that? Make us think we have to do all the things they didn't, or couldn't, do?"

"Don't your folks want you to have a dance career?"

"Yes, they've always supported me in my dancing, especially my dad. But now it's like I have to do things for Amy *and* me. For all the things she won't be able to do because she's gone. It kind of scares me, you know? What if I fail?"

Erin could feel David's fingers in her hair. "You can't fail at anything, Erin," he said.

A funny quiver shot through her stomach. "Why are you so nice to me, David, when I've been mean to you?"

"I like you. You're pretty. And you're a great dancer, so I respect your talent. You walk around like a princess, as if you've got everything under control." He stretched a curl, then coiled it around his finger. "But you don't, do you?"

His evaluation made her sigh. "I sure don't. My parents are hanging all over my life. If I'm even thirty minutes late, my mom is practically calling the police."

"Maybe they're scared of losing you too."

"Maybe so, but that's not fair to me. All I want to do is dance, go to school, and do things with friends. But most of my old friends pity me. Except Shara. She sort of understands."

"I hate it when people pity you. When Jody goes out in public, when people catch on to the fact that she's deaf, they either back off or start fawning over her. Both are insulting. They should just treat her like a regular kid."

Erin understood what he was saying. She'd experienced much of the same thing when people found out that Amy had died. They either avoided Erin altogether or said stupid things like, "I know exactly how you feel," or "At least she's not suffering"—as if death were preferable over suffering. "Do your parents fight a lot?" she asked.

"What do you mean?"

"Before Amy—" She stopped. "When we were all together, our family used to be happier and do stuff together. Picnics, dinner parties, my folks went out. Now everybody sort of goes separate ways. Mom used to love to cook, put together photo albums, things like that, but she doesn't anymore. She's busy with her store and all. But sometimes I wish things could be like they used to be." The warmth of David's body, the softness of the sand, and the low hum of the sea were making Erin drowsy. Her eyelids drooped.

"Are you feeling all right?" David asked.

She waved her hand. "I'm all right. I took my medicine."

"What medicine?"

Her eyes struggled open. Why had she told him? She hadn't meant to. She shifted in his arms and sat up straighter. "Sometimes I get these headaches."

"Like that day at the mall? I remember how sick you were. I was worried about you. So was Jody."

She wasn't sure she wanted him to worry about her. It meant one more person to try to please. "Why do you get them?" he asked.

"The doctors don't know." Erin paused, embarrassed to feel so exposed before him. "They've done a bunch of tests, but in the end they decided it was all in my mind. So now I'm seeing a counselor, and she's trying to figure out what's causing them." She hadn't meant to tell him about Dr. Richardson either.

"Is she helping at all?"

"I still have the headaches. I hope we have a breakthrough soon, because I've got plans to go to a special dance school this summer. I won't be able to go if I'm not well. And if I'm not well, then maybe I won't be able to go to Florida State in the fall either. I couldn't stand that, David."

"You're going away for the summer?" He sounded disappointed.

Without warning she grew agitated and struggled to her feet. "Maybe if I go away, I can get well. You know, not having to be around all the things that remind me of Amy could help me out. And being away from my parents might help too."

David rose next to her. "What does the counselor say?"

"Not much." She crossed her arms. "I'm supposed to be working through it. I sometimes don't want to go see her, but Mom freaks out if I don't."

She scrambled over the sand berm, saying, "I need to walk," and headed for the shoreline.

"Hey, wait up." In a moment David was next to her. "Slow down, this isn't a footrace."

Travis's voice said, "You know, I've suddenly got the urge to go for a run. At this hour you don't have to get out of the way for other joggers. Yeah, the world's pretty empty right now."

"Can't you keep up?" Erin asked David.

He caught her elbow. He'd rolled up the cuffs of his shirt, and his bow tie dangled around the open neck of the shirt. "Why're you running off? We were right in the middle of a discussion."

"I'm tired of talking," she said, pulling away and continuing down the beach. The tide was coming in, and waves kept lapping over her feet.

David stopped her again, taking both her elbows in his hands and drawing her close. "If you don't talk to me, how will I know what you're feeling?"

Ocean water sucked the sand away, and the sensation was one of being nibbled up by the ground. "I told you, I'm feeling all mixed up and crazy." She wasn't cold, but her teeth began to chatter. "Please let me go."

For a moment David didn't move; then slowly he released her and stepped backward. She watched him back off and felt lost. Behind her the sea pulled on the hem of her dress. "It was such a simple thing to do, you know? All she had to do was drive to the store and buy some sodas. Any moron could have done it. She knew how to drive too, you know. She told me she'd driven Travis's car, and it was a real racing machine—not like my old clunker.

"But she screwed it up. She waved good-bye, she drove off, and she never came back. I can still see the taillights of the car."

David came closer, and because the tide had eroded away so much sand from where she was standing, she was inches below him and had to look up to see his face. "She shouldn't have done that, David. I'm so *angry* at her!" Tears came, and Erin clenched her teeth. "She had no right to die. She h—had no r—right to—to—" Her voice shook, and her whole body trembled. "Why did she do it? Why did Amy go away and leave me all by myself?"

Chapter Fifteen

❧

Erin drifted on a sea of cozy, snuggly warmth and struggled to open her eyes. Light floated around her, and slowly she came to realize that she was on a sofa cushion on the floor of Shara's beach house. She rolled over and came face-to-face with a sleeping David.

She instantly sat up, only to see that she was surrounded by many sleeping couples. They were curled and bunched next to one another on cushions and pillows spread across the floor. Crumpled taffeta and crushed satin gave the room an eerie look, as if a magic spell had been cast and people had simply dropped in their tracks.

Erin's muscles ached from sleeping on the floor. She arched her back and rubbed her arms. Carefully she studied David. How childlike he looked as the sunlight pouring in through sliding glass doors turned his hair the color of spun gold. Erin watched him, trying to remember the evening before.

It returned in snatches, like scraps of photographs tossed into the wind. Walking the beach with David and crying . . . sitting in the sand while

David rocked her . . . coming back to the house only when the music had stopped and the lights had gone out . . . stepping over bodies stretched along the floor, and David wrestling a sofa cushion from someone already asleep . . . David pulling her down next to him and holding her until the rhythmic sound of others breathing had lulled her into an exhausted sleep.

She'd made a fool of herself the night before. Why had she started talking about Amy in the first place? Why had she broken down and cried? Where had all the anger and tears come from? *Maybe it was the medication,* she told herself. Yes, that had to be it. She'd taken the pills to stave off a headache, and they must have caused her to "lose it" in front of David. How could she face him today?

Quietly Erin rose and carefully threaded her way into the bathroom. Once there, she stared at her reflection in the mirror, at her tangled hair and mascara-smudged eyes, still red and swollen. God, she looked awful! She wondered where her purse was and her hairbrush. She splashed water on her face and rinsed her mouth. She needed some orange juice and decided to go to the kitchen.

Pinky and Andy and three other couples were sitting at the pine table talking quietly.

Pinky grinned. "Did we wake you guys?" Her eyes were glassy, and Erin realized that this group hadn't slept at all.

"No. Is there any juice?"

"Help yourself." Erin took the paper cup Andy

shoved toward her. She found the juice in the refrigerator and filled the cup.

"Some party, huh?" Pinky asked. "Where'd you and David spend the evening?" There was an innuendo in Pinky's voice that Erin didn't like.

"We just walked the beach."

"Uh-huh . . ." Pinky drawled, cutting her eyes toward Andy.

Erin didn't care what they thought. She was exhausted and wanted to go home, take a shower, and sleep in her own bed. "What time is it anyway?" she asked.

"Seven o'clock."

The last time Erin remembered seeing a clock, it had been four A.M. "Short night," she said, draining the last of her juice.

"I'm glad Ms. Thornton said no play practice today," Pinky said.

The play. Inwardly Erin groaned. The performance was a week from Saturday, and suddenly she was dreading it, as if it were too big a chore to tackle.

"Hi, guys. What's for breakfast?" David stepped through the doorway.

"Whatever you want to fix," Pinky told him, and everybody laughed.

He tried to catch Erin's eye, but she refused. He'd seen her soul last night, and now, in the light of day, she felt more exposed than if she'd stood before him naked.

"You don't think I can cook?" David said, stepping around her. "What do you want? Eggs, French toast, pancakes? Just name it."

"How about cereal?" Seth said, sauntering into the room. "It's hard to screw that up."

"Ye of little faith," David said. "Watch this, hair ball." In minutes he had everyone organized, and eggs were being scrambled, toast was browning, and the aroma was bringing other sleepy kids into the kitchen.

Erin stood aside, impressed by the way David could take over a room, grateful that she didn't have to interact with anybody. Later he drove her home, but she avoided talking by feigning sleep, and at her front door he asked, "Can I call you later?"

"I'm gonna crash for the rest of the day. I'll see you at play practice Monday after school." She went inside before he could say anything else.

Her mother was waiting for her inside the door. "Did you have fun? Are you all right?" She was trying to sound pleasant, but Erin saw the circles under her eyes and realized that she'd probably been up most of the night too.

"I'm fine, Mom. I told you not to worry."

"I wasn't worrying. I was just asking. Can't I even ask if you had a good time or not?"

Erin felt guilty, but she was too tired to hassle with her mother. "Can I tell you all about it later? I'm really wiped out."

"Yes, of course. Go on to bed and we can talk tonight."

"Are you working today? Should I start dinner?"

"We'll go out for dinner."

"Where's Daddy?"

"Out. He said he'd be out tonight too. No use in cooking for just the two of us."

"No use," she agreed. "No use at all."

"Erin, it's really great to see you. I'm so glad you called and wanted to come over." Beth Wilson's eyes shone as she spoke.

Erin sat cross-legged on Beth's bed, munching popcorn. "I've been wanting to come over for ages, but with school and play practice and Spring Fling and all—"

"How was the dance? Tell me about it."

Erin still wasn't caught up on her rest, but Sunday afternoon at her house had been filled with its usual tension, so she'd called Beth and practically invited herself over. "The dance was fun, and afterward we stayed up all night at Shara's beach house. We all sort of fell asleep together on the floor."

Beth clutched her knees and giggled. "Sounds romantic."

Erin recalled how snuggly and content she'd felt in David's arms. "Hardly," she said. "My bones still hurt from the hard floor. I'd never make a camper."

"We used to camp," Beth said wistfully. "Before my mom got real sick. Before Dad left."

"How is your mom?"

Beth shrugged. "About the same. She has to go for dialysis again every other day, and they're trying to locate another donor kidney for her."

Beth's house smelled of sickness. Erin noticed it as soon as Beth opened the front door, but she smiled and came inside anyway. It reminded her too much of the hospital, of the Neuro-ICU unit, and of Amy's cubicle. "Then they'll do a second transplant?" she asked.

"Yeah, just as soon as they find a donor kidney with a good tissue match. Of course, there's no telling how long that will take, so all we can do is wait and continue the dialysis. But Mom's a priority. You know how it is."

Erin knew how it was. Somebody had to die in order that somebody else could go on living. *"You can't just turn off the machines. You can't just give Amy away in bits and pieces,"* she had pleaded with her parents.

Her mother had said, *"Something has to make sense. Organ donation is our only way of making this whole thing plausible."*

"So," Beth was saying, "how's your love life?"

Erin blushed. "What love life?"

"You know—David Devlin? Didn't you have fun with him Friday night?"

"David's all right."

"Just all right?"

Erin studied a spot on the wall, above Beth's head. "I don't know why everybody's trying to fix me up with David. It's not like that between us. He's just a guy I do things with. That's all."

"Gosh, Erin, I didn't mean to make you mad. I was only teasing."

"And I didn't mean to snap," Erin said. "It's the play and finals coming up. I don't know. I guess it's just me."

"And I'm trying to live vicariously," Beth admitted with a quick smile. "Because my life's the pits."

"Are you going to finish the school year?"

"I have to. When Mom found out I was skipping classes to help around here, she exploded. For a sick woman she really let loose. But even though I'm finishing high school, I refuse to go away to college."

"Will you go at all?"

"Just to Hillsborough Junior College. That way I can be at home, look after Mom and my brother and sisters, and still get some sort of college degree."

Erin was counting the days until she could go away and start living on her own—if only her parents would let her. She felt sorry for Beth. It didn't seem fair that she was having to give up her plans all because her father decided he couldn't cope with having a sick wife. "Has your dad ever called or written?"

Beth shook her head. "But we do have some help financially now, and I don't think Social Services is going to break up our family. A social worker with the dialysis unit figured out that things weren't going so hot for us, and she's been a big help. She checks on us every week, and so far I've been able to convince her that I'm doing a good job."

To Erin it seemed as if Beth were doing a superb job. "You are coming to the play, aren't you?"

"I'm planning on it. How's it going?"

"You know how it is toward the end of rehearsals—it seems like a disaster, but somehow it all comes together at the last minute, and you make it through. We've got dress rehearsals all this week."

Beth looked disappointed. "I was hoping that maybe we could go to a movie or something Friday night."

Erin wanted to tell Beth that the big rehearsal was all day Saturday and that she would be free Friday night. But she'd made up her mind to do something else on Friday night.

Maybe losing it in front of David on the beach was what finally pushed her into it. Maybe it was the stark, raw anguish she kept remembering from that night when she'd shouted about how angry she was at Amy for dying. Erin didn't know. She only knew she wanted to be happy again and think about dancing and college and her future. She wanted to be free of headaches and ghosts and the past.

"We'll do something as soon as this play's over, all right?"

"You're on," Beth said with a grin.

Erin had decided to attend Dr. Richardson's grief support group meeting on Friday night. She would hear what others her own age had to say who'd lost family members. For a moment she was once again tempted to tell Beth about her therapy sessions. And even though it would be nice to bring a friend along to the group meeting, Erin figured it was something she really should do on her own. Besides, Beth seemed to be doing all right now, especially because of the social worker she'd mentioned.

Debriding the wound, Dr. Richardson had called it. Erin winced, thinking of the emotional pain that lay ahead of her. Was there really no magic balm?

Chapter Sixteen

~

"It's good to see so many of you here tonight," Dr. Richardson said. "And a special welcome to you newcomers."

Erin looked nervously around the circle of chairs set up in Dr. Richardson's conference room. She managed a self-conscious smile, certain that she was the only newcomer there. Ten other kids nodded, waved, and said hi. They all looked normal to her. *What did you expect?* she asked herself. *Do people who've lost family members wear marks on their foreheads?*

"I've ordered pizza for everyone after tonight's session," Dr. Richardson said, and a cheer went up. "Will somebody tell me what kind of a week he or she had?"

Silence fell on the room, until an overweight boy of about twelve spoke. "My mom found the box of Twinkies I hid under my bed and blew up."

"Why'd you hide them there?" a girl asked. "That's the first place my mom always cleans."

The boy shrugged. "I shouldn't have had them, I guess."

"Then why did you?" someone asked.

"My dad and I used to sneak into the kitchen at

night when everybody was asleep, and sometimes we'd eat Twinkies together. I kind of feel like he's still around when I eat them."

"Sounds like an excuse to pig out to me," a girl said with disdain.

The fat boy leapt from his chair. "That's a rotten thing to say, Michelle! Take it back!"

Dr. Richardson interrupted. "But, Todd, you've been telling us for weeks that you want to lose weight. How can you if you sneak Twinkies?"

"I told you, it makes me feel like my dad's still alive."

"Well, I wish I *could* eat," another girl said. "But my stomach's upset all the time. All my mother does is try to push food on me."

"I'll trade you," Todd told her. "All my mom does is yell at me."

Erin listened as others talked, feeling close to them even though they were strangers. A thirteen-year-old boy named Benjie said, "After my baby brother died in his crib last summer, my mom sort of freaked out too. She started staying in bed all day and cried all the time. Dad always had to make supper, but we just sat looking at each other at the table. He wasn't a very good cook.

"Once I sneaked into the baby's room, but it gave me the creeps. Everything was just the same, except the baby was gone. It was like everybody kept expecting him to come home. I really wished Mom would put his things away. I stepped on one of his rattles by accident and broke it, and Mom slapped me. I cried. But I didn't want to, because I'm too old to cry."

His story sent shivers up Erin's spine as she remembered the boxes and trunk stored in the garage. And now that Amy's bedroom was her mother's office, it seemed as if Amy had hardly lived with them at all.

"You know what gets me?" Kristy, a fifteen-year-old, said. "When my mom died of cancer, people came up to me and said, 'The good die young.' Was that supposed to make me feel better? Is dying some sort of reward for being good? If so, then I'm gonna be bad!"

Erin sympathized with Kristy's anger. After Amy had died, some adults had told her, "Amy was so special that God must have wanted her with Him." Erin had held her tongue, but she'd wanted to shout, "God's got the entire world to choose from, and I've only got one sister. So why did He have to pick *her*?"

"The things people say at funerals and wakes often do sound pretty empty," Dr. Richardson said. "But expressing sympathy is an awkward thing to do, and it takes a lot of courage. At least the people who said something cared enough about you and your family to try."

Dr. Richardson looked over at one boy who had propped his booted feet on an empty chair. "What do you think about being good, Charlie?"

Erin studied Charlie's sullen expression, his black leather jacket, and his unkempt hair. "Oh, I'm real good, Doc. Just ask Terry Parker. I made it with her real good last night."

"That's disgusting," Kristy said.

"I can make it real good for you too, babe. Want to meet in my car after this is over?"

"That'll do, Charlie," Dr. Richardson said quietly.

Charlie dropped his feet with a thud and leaned forward. "Look, I'm here because the judge says I gotta be here. I don't care about this little goody-goody group."

"Good for you," Todd said. "But the rest of us want to be here."

"Butt out, Tubb-o."

Dr. Richardson calmly shook her head. "I won't allow name calling, Charlie. We're here to build one another up. If you can't be polite—"

Charlie stood abruptly and crossed to the door. "I'm out of here. Give my share of the pizza to Fatso." He left, and Dr. Richardson excused herself and followed him.

For a moment no one spoke, and Erin could hear the clock humming on the wall. "Uh—what was his problem?" she finally asked.

Kristy fiddled with her bracelets. "He was driving drunk and hit another car head-on. His cousin was killed, and the guy in the other car is crippled for life."

Erin's eyes grew wide. "That's awful."

"Yeah," Kristy agreed. "And Charlie walked away without a scratch. I guess that's why we put up with him. He's hurting like crazy. He made a bad mistake, and he can't change it. One time he sort of broke down and cried in front of us and said he wished it was him who'd died."

The boy who'd been sitting next to Charlie added, "'Course it wasn't, but Charlie keeps acting so hateful that maybe someday somebody will do him the favor of taking him out."

Erin shuddered. There was so much anger and guilt and pain in the room, and she wondered how she fit into it. She thought back to the night of Amy's accident.

"What was she doing driving in the rain at night anyway?" her mother had demanded.

"I let her take my car."

"Why? Amy's not an experienced driver. I've always counted on you, Erin, to have common sense."

The door to the conference room opened, and Dr. Richardson came back in. "Charlie's all right," she assured them. "He'll be back next week."

"Whoopie," Todd said sarcastically.

They talked some more, and the session passed quickly, and afterward, when the pizza arrived, she noticed Todd greedily grab for the first slice. Erin took a piece too, but she didn't really want it. Her appetite had fled much as Charlie had. And worse, a tightening sensation was starting up the back of her neck. It was good to be around kids her age with similar problems, but not if it brought on a headache. She'd tell Dr. Richardson at her next counseling session that it was doubtful she could ever come back.

*   *   *

The backstage area was in chaos. The final performance of *West Side Story* had come off beautifully, and the applause of the audience still rang in Erin's ears. "Weren't we sensational?" Shara shouted, giving her a hug.

"Next stop, Broadway," Erin called.

People swarmed around them, offering congratulations. Erin felt euphoric, but then performing always gave her a "high." The cast kept telling her how good she and David had been. Erin kept smiling, searching the crowd for Beth, who didn't seem to be there.

David nudged his way through the masses, scooped Erin up in his arms, and twirled her around. "Not too shabby, 'Maria.' So what do you say we change and head for the cast party?"

"I—uh—I'm not going."

He looked stricken. "What?"

"No . . . I can't go."

"Why?"

"My folks are sort of paranoid, and they want me to come straight home. Cast parties have a bad reputation in our family. We were having a cast party the night Amy had the accident." Erin knew she was telling a half truth. *She* was the one who didn't want to go.

"Look, Erin, this might not be the time to bring it up, but you've been dodging me ever since the Spring Fling dance."

"That's not true," she protested, but knew it was.

David pulled her to a more secluded area of the stage and took her by the shoulders. "What's wrong?"

"I told you."

"What's wrong between you and me? I mean, when we were on the beach together, you were so open and honest."

"I sort of lost it that night, David. It wasn't supposed to be that way. Too much pressure—the play and all."

"Well, the play's over."

Erin's heart thudded, and she avoided his eyes. "I know. And that means that I won't be seeing much of you anymore."

"But I want to see you."

"Look, David, think about it. School will be out in a few more weeks, and this summer I'm probably going away, and even if I don't, I *will* be going to FSU in the fall. What's the point of us seeing each other?"

"What's the point? The point is, I care about you, Erin, and I want to be with you. I thought you were beginning to care about me too."

"Oh, I do like you." She said it too quickly, and David gave her a skeptical glance. "I just don't want to start something I can't finish."

"Like dating me?"

"You'll always be a special friend." *What a stupid, juvenile remark,* she told herself as soon as the words were out. Nothing was going the way Erin had planned. She didn't want to hurt David, and she didn't want to feel about him the way she did either. She glanced around. "Everybody's starting to leave. I—uh—I'd better get going."

David took her arm. His hurt expression had been replaced with one of determination. "You need me, Erin. No matter what you say otherwise, it's as simple as that."

She blinked, speechless. *Of all the conceited, arrogant*—she jerked her arm free. "I'm getting out of this city as soon as I can. I don't need anybody." His grin started, and he backed up slowly. "You think that's *funny?*" she shouted.

"I told you once that clowns see the humor in everything. The good and the bad."

"Well then, go ahead and laugh!" Erin was furious. She watched him walk away, and the last thing she heard was his whistling.

Erin moped around the house Sunday afternoon, feeling lost. She'd done her homework, TV was boring, her father was gone for the day, and her mother was driving her crazy with dumb questions about dumb things. She still wasn't over her argument with David either. And as much as she hated to admit it, she missed him and wished she hadn't handled things so badly the night before.

She was grateful when the phone rang. "Erin? It's me, Beth." Her friend's voice sounded small and tight.

"What's wrong?"

"We got the call this morning. They have a kidney for my mother. I'm at the hospital right now, and they're prepping her for surgery. Can you please come and wait with me?"

Chapter Seventeen

For Erin, walking back into the seventh-floor waiting room at the hospital was like stepping through a time warp. Memories of the days she spent by Amy's side overwhelmed her, and she almost fled, but out of the sea of anxious faces of people waiting for news of family and friends, she heard Beth call her.

Quickly Erin swallowed her emotions and took a chair next to her friend. "Any news yet?" she asked.

"They just started the surgery. It'll take several hours."

"Last time they flew her to Gainesville. Why not this time?"

"She has another doctor. And this hospital has a transplant team now too. It's better they don't have to fly her out this time anyway so we can all be near her. Jason's at the next-door neighbor's," she explained. "He's not real aware of what's going on because he's only six. He just knows Mom's sick and the operation is supposed to make her better."

Erin was struck with the irony of the situation. Here was Beth trying to be an anchor for her family, while Erin felt more like a burden to hers. Her sister had lingered in a coma, trapped in a mysterious universe between life and death; Beth's mother was still alive, but if the transplant wasn't successful, then she would be dead too.

"I think Amy would have approved of us donating her organs," Erin said slowly, recalling how bitterly opposed she'd been to the idea at the time. But agreeing to donation meant turning off the machines and admitting that Amy was dead. Erin supposed that *that* was the part that had been the hardest for her.

"I checked the place on my driver's license to be a donor if I die in an accident," Beth said. "It seems sort of wasteful to bury a body whose organs could go to help somebody who's still alive."

The direction of the conversation was giving Erin the creeps, so she asked if anyone wanted a soda and then went to the machine. "I don't want to be here," she mumbled to herself as she opened the canned drink. There was an ache deep inside her throat she couldn't wash away with the soda. She saw a pay phone on the wall and thought about the time she'd called Travis and he'd come to the hospital to visit Amy. Of course, he couldn't deal with being in the cubicle with her comatose sister, and so he left and never visited again. Erin hadn't forgiven him for that either.

"David," she whispered, and suddenly she wanted him with her. She needed his smile and positive attitude. She dialed his number from the pay phone, and once she explained where she was and what she was doing there, he said, "I'll be right over."

He arrived within thirty minutes, and the familiar sight of him strolling into the area—hands thrust into the pockets of his baggy Bermudas, and his shirt looking as if it needed to be ironed—made her want to run up and throw her arms around him. Of course, she didn't.

"Thanks for coming," Erin said.

He flipped his blond hair off his forehead and flashed the smile she knew so well. "Thanks for asking."

In no time he'd tracked down the board game Aggravation from one of the nurses, and soon all of them were huddled around the board in a corner of the waiting area. Beth's sister Willa rolled the dice, landed on David's game piece, and sent him home to start all over again. She giggled and clapped her hands.

"I'm a terrible loser," David told the little girl, then reached over and produced her game piece magically from behind her ear.

Willa stared at the empty spot on the board where her playing piece had been. "How'd you do that?"

"You mean this?" David pulled Beth's game piece from behind her other ear. "Or this?" He opened a closed fist, and there lay Erin's and Jill's Aggravation marbles.

By now Willa's eyes were shining. "That's neat!"

David turned to Erin. "See, I told you women under the age of ten love me."

"I never doubted it," Erin said with a laugh.

"It's the ones over ten I have all my problems with." He turned back to an awestruck Willa and asked, "Would you like a dog?" He reached in his pocket and pulled out a balloon. Moments later he'd blown it up and sculpted it into a dachshund.

By now a small crowd had collected. He made other balloon animals and passed them out, and when someone handed him a deck of cards, he performed several amazing sleight-of-hand tricks.

Finally he announced, "That's about it, folks." The small gathering applauded. It surprised Erin to see that an hour had passed. He took her elbow and asked, "How about we go down to the cafeteria for some supper?"

Beth urged them to go, and once downstairs David bought their dinners and found a table near a long row of windows. Outside, twilight had fallen. "Thanks for breaking the monotony up there," Erin told him. "You really took people's minds off their worries."

"I'm a natural show-off, remember? Collecting an audience is my strong suit."

"Still, you made everybody forget their gloom and doom." She took a bite of her hamburger. "You also do a pretty good show—but don't let it go to your head."

David feigned a fainting spell. "I can't believe it! Erin thinks I'm a good act."

"Don't be a wise guy."

"Well, it so happens that I've got some news for you about my plans this summer. Since you're going off to dance school, I'm trying to get into clown school."

Erin looked blank. "'Clown school'? You can take *classes* for clowning?"

"It's part of the Ringling Circus's permanent quarters down in Sarasota, and it puts out some of the world's top clowns. I haven't been accepted yet, but since you'll be gone, why stick around here? The summer program starts in June, after the Special Olympics. You sure I can't persuade you to help out at the games?"

"Not this year. And by the way, going away to Wolftrap isn't a sure thing for me either. Dr. Richardson has to okay it and persuade my parents I'm well enough to go."

"Why wouldn't she?"

"The headaches. I'm a lot better," Erin added quickly. "But even if I was one hundred percent, my parents are dragging their feet about my going. They hate to let me out of their sight."

"Like the night of the cast party?"

Erin swallowed, remembering how she'd hurt David's feelings by not going. "They're practically smothering me to death, David. In fact, we're all supposed to meet in Dr. Richardson's office this Saturday to talk about the course of my treatment and all."

"What treatment?" Beth asked, startling them both.

"We didn't hear you come up," Erin said. "Is everything all right?"

"Mom's out of surgery, and they've taken her down to ICU. Her doctor says it went real well, and that the new kidney is functioning fine. 'Course, the next few days will tell us a lot more. Now, why are you going to a doctor? You never told me *you* were sick. I couldn't take it if you were sick too, Erin."

"No, no, it's nothing like that," Erin said.

"Here, sit down." David pulled out a chair for her.

Erin had never meant for anybody to know she was seeing a therapist, and now both David and Beth knew. She took a deep breath and told Beth about the headaches and the visits to Dr. Richardson.

Beth listened intently. "Gosh, Erin. I never would have guessed. I mean, I thought you had it all together. You seem so sure of yourself and so composed. I was the one who was falling apart."

"Well, looks can be deceiving," she confessed. David reached out and took her hand, and the simple gesture almost unraveled her. "Sometimes I guess we all need somebody to share things with."

"I know it helps me now to talk things out with the social worker," Beth admitted. "But before her, I had you to share my feelings with."

"And I never felt like I was much help to you."

"That's not true. I'll never forget the day we ended up shopping for your prom dress. It was fun, and I sure needed the break."

David's grip tightened, and he said, "Look, if everything's all right for you and your sisters now, Erin and I will go. We've both got school tomorrow."

"Oh, sure," Beth said. She hugged Erin when they all stood up. "I'll never forget the two of you being here for us."

"Call me and let me know how your mom's doing," Erin said, suddenly light-headed.

Beth promised, then hurried away. David put his arm around Erin, and she let him lead her out of the hospital and into the parking lot. Night had fallen, but the air was humid and muggy. She smelled rain. "You're not feeling good, are you?" he asked.

"How did you know?"

His arm tightened. "I'm clairvoyant. And besides, your face is the color of a sheet."

"Oh, David." She leaned against him. "I don't think I'm ever going to get well."

"I'll drive you home."

"But my car—"

"I'll get it back to you later tonight."

Thunder rumbled, and the breeze picked up. She clung to David, and when large drops of water began to spatter, she didn't even care. He pulled her under a covered walkway. "We'll have to wait until it lets up," he said. "Then we'll make a dash to my car."

She rested her cheek on his chest and listened as the drumming rain mingled with the sound of his heartbeat. The scents of wet grass and asphalt

blended with the scent of his soap and cologne.
With her arms locked around his waist, Erin looked
up into David's face. Light from the parking-lot
lamps bathed him in gold. David made a circle with
his open hand in front of her face, then ran his
thumb along her jaw. The signed gesture told her,
pretty girl. Her pulse fluttered, racing with the
rhythm of the rain. She closed her eyes as he
cupped her chin and kissed her tenderly on the
lips.

Chapter Eighteen

❦

Dr. Richardson's office seemed smaller to Erin now that her mother and father were with her. They were sitting on a sofa, with Erin in a chair next to it, and Dr. Richardson in a chair in front of them.

"I don't see why we have to be here," Mrs. Bennett said.

"Because we want to help Erin," Mr. Bennett told her, as if she were a not-too-bright child.

Erin felt a tightness clamp like bands around her temples. Surely her parents wouldn't have a fight right in front of the counselor!

Dr. Richardson said, "I know you've been concerned about Erin's headaches. When one person hurts, the whole family hurts. Can you tell me how her headaches affected you?"

Mrs. Bennett said, "We've done everything we could—we've spent a fortune on tests—and frankly, I don't believe she's a whole lot better now in spite of her therapy sessions."

"But I *am* better!" Erin blurted. "They don't come on nearly as often."

"But you still have them," her mother said.

"Erin wants to take a dance scholarship this

143

summer," Mr. Bennett commented, as if the exchange between Erin and his wife hadn't occurred. "And she wants to go away to college in the fall, but with these headaches and all—"

Mrs. Bennett interrupted. "I don't see how that's possible. She'd be far away, and if she got sick, who would take care of her?" Erin's heart ached because she wasn't sure how she'd survive if she couldn't go away. "She's all we have you know, and—"

"You have each other," Erin exclaimed. Her parents stared directly at the counselor, as if she hadn't spoken.

"Erin doesn't understand how nervous we get over her moving away. She needs me when she's sick. . . . Why, she can barely function."

"But sometimes I feel like I'm in the way," Erin said, twisting her hands in her lap as the pressure mounted inside her head. "You have your store and all."

"My work helps me. It keeps me busy and my mind on other things."

"If you didn't have the store, and didn't have to worry about Erin's headaches, what do you think life would be like?" Dr. Richardson asked.

Mrs. Bennett toyed with an earring and stared evasively into space. "I'm sure you understand what a difficult year this has been for all of us."

"Because your daughter died?"

"Yes, because my daughter died! Whenever Erin's sick, whenever I'm busy at the store, I don't have time to—to—" She stopped, and Dr.

Richardson let the silence stretch until Erin began to perspire. She wanted someone to jump in and finish her mother's sentence for her sake. "Well, it's just easier to go on from day to day if I'm busy."

"Dad works a lot too," Erin said.

"Do you work a lot?" Dr. Richardson asked.

Mr. Bennett cleared his throat. "I've found work to be therapeutic. I keep occupied."

"He retreats," Mrs. Bennett said. "There's a difference." He glared at her, as if she'd exposed him in some way.

The therapist turned to Erin. "And what do you do?"

"I've already told you—I go to school, dance, and work in Mom's store. We all keep busy."

"And what do you do together as a family?"

"Not much."

"Why?"

Erin sat on her hands. "We're not a family anymore."

Her mother gasped. "How can you say such a thing? Of course we're a family."

"When Amy was alive, we did things together. Now we don't. We don't sit around the table and eat and laugh like we used to either." Amy used to make them all laugh. Erin supposed that there was nothing left to laugh about now. She thought of David's clowning and of how he made her laugh.

"But things are different now," Dr. Richardson said. "You're all trying to find ways of dealing with the great loss you've experienced. It seems to me as

though you haven't given yourselves time to grieve
fully."

"We've grieved," Mrs. Bennett said, holding
her head erect and blinking. "Now we're just trying
to go on with life."

"Grieving is a process with many stages," Dr.
Richardson said. "It's intricate and involved, and I
want to help you through it. You're wise to use
therapy to support the family while you work your
way through the thoughts and feelings about Amy's
death."

Erin squirmed in her chair. She didn't want to
talk about Amy's death. She wanted Dr. Richardson
to convince her parents that she was well enough to
move away. "So why don't they want me to go away
this summer? It's like they're punishing me."

Her father leaned toward her. "Honey, you're
not being punished. You haven't done anything
wrong."

"Mom said I did." Erin surprised herself with
her sudden comment.

"When? I've never said such a thing!"

"Yes, I heard you. When I first came to the
hospital after Amy's accident. You told me that I
never should have let Amy go to the store because
she'd just gotten her license and wasn't very experienced." Erin's voice sounded angry and ashamed.

"But I never—I mean, I was upset."

"It was an accident," her father added.

Erin looked at them, from one face to the
other, and nodded vigorously. "But you were right.
I shouldn't have let her go, but I really didn't want

to go myself, and so I let her have her way. Why did I do that?"

Dr. Richardson said, "You're angry because she talked you into it."

"Yes, I let her have her way! If *I* had gone on the errand instead of Amy, then the accident never would have happened!"

"But it was raining. Could you have stopped the rain?"

Erin felt flushed all over. She twisted in her chair. "Of course I couldn't."

"So what if you had lost control of the car too? Then what would have happened?"

"I—I would have been the one who died."

"But you're a more experienced driver. You might have had better control of the skid," Dr. Richardson reasoned. "Erin, don't you see what you've done? You've built a whole case—served as judge and jury for yourself—based on 'if only.' If only *I* had driven instead. If only it hadn't been raining. If only I hadn't let her talk me into driving to the store."

"But my mother said—"

"You've beat yourself up for the last year over something you had no control over."

"But I let her drive, and she wasn't experienced," Erin insisted. Why couldn't Dr. Richardson understand that she really *was* to blame for Amy's death?

"Your sister was a sixteen-year-old licensed driver. She'd taken a driver's test and was approved for a legal license. *She* was driving the car. *She* knew how to drive. *She* lost control. It was an accident."

"But I *feel* so responsible. Because I was the 'responsible one,' and Amy was the baby. Isn't that right?" Erin couldn't help crying now as she turned to her parents. "Amy'll never get to be an actress." She looked at her father, whose eyes were brimming. "She'll never get to grow up." She looked at her mother, whose face was the color of paste.

Gently Dr. Richardson said, "Erin, this is guilt you're feeling—a natural part of grieving. It's good that you're allowing yourself to express it. It's okay to forgive yourself for something that wasn't your fault."

"Sometimes I feel so depressed." Erin blew her nose. "I feel like I'm going crazy, like I have to do it all, because Amy's gone."

"Letting these tears and feelings out will ensure that you won't go crazy. In fact, I believe that your headaches are a result of keeping these feelings bottled up inside."

Dr. Richardson faced Erin's parents. "Erin's been trying to help both of you, to distract you from your pain. She's carried on, tried to take up the slack and act as a buffer, and yet still plan for a future. The headaches are a reflection of the terrible strain she's under. It's tough being the glue that holds everybody together."

"We never meant for that to happen," Mr. Bennett said, shaking his head.

Dr. Richardson continued. "Erin's headaches have been the focus of your lives this past year. I believe that if both of you would come in for separate counseling as well as together as a family, you'll all be able to work out your grief and put the pieces back together again."

"But we're working things out," Mrs. Bennett protested, crying openly.

"As parents you're facing a double loss: Amy's death—an unnatural event—and Erin's growing up and leaving home—a natural one. It can be scary facing the unknown. Yet Erin has to feel that the two of you are going to be all right before she can afford to be well and achieve her goals."

"So you're saying that we're partly to blame for Erin's headaches," Mr. Bennett commented, shifting in his chair.

Her mother wept. "I never meant to blame you, Erin. Never!"

Erin buried her face in her hands. She felt her future and all her dreams slipping away. She felt tired and defeated. "I won't go away if you really don't want me to," she whispered.

"That's not a decision we have to make right now," Dr. Richardson said kindly. "Right now we need to focus on all of you getting your feelings out. You need to confront your anger, fear, and guilt. Then we can discuss the future."

Erin raised tearstained eyes to her parents. They were crying too, but it didn't embarrass her. She half wished she was a little girl again and could curl up in their laps and be soothed. "I want things to be like they were before Amy died," she said.

"That's impossible," her father said.

"I agree," Dr. Richardson told them. "But things can be good again. You can be a happy and unified family if we work together on your healing. Today has given you an excellent beginning."

Erin watched her parents glance at one another, then nod in agreement. She rubbed the back of her neck, but the dull ache was already starting to subside.

Chapter Nineteen

~~~

Erin watched the rain from her living-room window. The water splattered against the glass, then ran in rivulets, pooled and collected on the outside sill before running off the edges and into the shrubbery. Her insides felt as liquid as the rain. Ever since her family's session with Dr. Richardson, she'd cried off and on until she was sure that she was empty, that there couldn't possibly be one more tear left within her. And that made her task for this afternoon a little bit easier.

Erin turned and crossed to the middle of the floor where Amy's trunk sat waiting. The house was silent, because both her parents were at a counseling session, and since classes and exams were finally over, she had nothing else to do but sort through her sister's things. Dr. Richardson had told her, "I believe it will help heal you." Now she realized that more than her headaches needed healing. Her parents needed healing too.

Erin sat on the sofa, reached out, and unsnapped the catch on the trunk. She raised the lid. Clothing lay on top—Amy's favorite items. She lifted a red blouse and remembered the day Amy had bought it.

She'd said, "Erin, can you loan me the money for this. Please . . . I'll be your best friend."

Beneath the clothing she found the case Amy had received for her sixteenth birthday to hold her clown makeup. Amy had been delighted because she thought it made her look like a "real pro." Erin smiled, because on the first opportunity Amy had had to carry it—the dance recital—she'd forgotten it. Erin opened the kit and examined the tubes of greasepaint.

She unscrewed one cap, closed her eyes, and sniffed. The heavy, oily odor sent her back to the Children's Home and the day she'd filled in for Amy and had first met David.

Funny how they'd met again during the play. David had turned out to be as zany in real life as he'd been that day he'd entertained the children. So much like Amy. Erin still wondered why she never told him about their *real* first meeting. But now that they were going their separate ways for the summer, she guessed it didn't matter anymore.

Erin remembered his kiss and touched her mouth. *No use getting all sentimental*, she told herself, closing the lid of the makeup case and snapping the catch tightly. David was a part of the past now too. Time to go forward.

Inside the trunk she discovered a shoe box filled with photographs. There was a strip of her and Amy they'd taken one day at the mall in one of those "instant-photo" machines. In one frame Amy had crossed her eyes and Erin was looking exasperated. In another Amy had sneezed just as the camera had fired.

And there were photos of Amy and Travis—of the two of them beside a Christmas tree, kissing under mistletoe, and sitting in Travis's sports car.

Erin ran her fingers over the glossy surfaces, tracing her sister's smiling face locked in time, forever young. A lump swelled in her throat, so she quickly shoved the photos back into the box and put it aside.

She found a pile of gifts and keepsakes from Travis—a necklace with a single pearl, his Christmas gift to her, a football pennant, several ticket stubs, and a broken comb. "You sure kept some weird things," Erin said aloud. But then she supposed that she would have done the same thing if Travis had given them to her.

She uncovered the teddy bear Travis had given Amy in the hospital—the one Erin had tried to give back to him the night he'd dated Cindy. She'd come very close to throwing it into the bay but in the end had brought it home to Amy's room.

She hugged the tattered bear, burying her face in its fur. It smelled of Amy's perfume. She pulled the familiar bottle out of the trunk and spritzed its fragrance into the air. The scent was light and floral. She closed her eyes and inhaled.

After a few moments Erin opened her eyes again. She was alone—yet, surrounded by all of Amy's belongings, it had seemed—just for a moment—that Amy had been there too. "What do you

think, Mr. Bear? What should we do with Amy's
things? If we give them away, someone else will just
toss them. If we keep them—" She stopped because her eyes were misting over, and her throat
had clogged up again. If she kept them, someday
she'd be able to tell her children all about Aunt
Amy. She'd be able to let them meet Amy in a different sort of way.

Slowly she gathered up the mementos and
packed them lovingly back inside the trunk. She'd
save everything, and she'd have her father put the
trunk in her bedroom, at the foot of her bed. And
the trunk, and all it contents, would be hers for all
time, and somehow that meant Amy would be too.

She closed the lid and leaned her head against
the sofa. Outside, the rain had slackened, and the
sun was struggling through the cloud cover. Dr.
Richardson had been right. It had helped to touch
her sister this way. She felt better inside. And now
she had just one more thing to do. One more task
before she could close this chapter on her life and
begin the next one.

Erin got up and went to the kitchen and picked
up the phone.

"I'd like to speak to Travis Sinclair, please."

The guy on the other end said, "Let me check
his room."

The receiver clunked down, and Erin heard
him yell, "Hey, Travis, some babe's on the phone!"
The sounds of the college dorm, of male voices and
doors slamming, filled Erin's ear. In a few minutes

the receiver was picked up, and Travis's voice said, "Yeah?"

Erin almost lost her courage. Her palms began to sweat, the receiver becoming slippery in her hand. "Travis? It—it's Erin Bennett."

There was a long pause. "Where are you?"

"Tampa. Home."

"How'd you get my number?"

"I called your mom and asked her for it."

"What do you want, Erin?"

What *did* she want? "I think I want to tell you that I'm sorry."

"Sorry about what?"

"Sorry about . . . the way I treated you, you know, last year when Amy was . . . was . . ."

"It was a hard time for all of us," Travis said quickly. "It's all right, I understand."

"And then that day we met at the mall. I'm sorry about that too."

"I probably shouldn't have spoken to you. I knew how you felt. But when I saw you, I just remembered Amy so strong. It was like she might have been there with you."

Erin leaned against the kitchen wall because her knees were trembling. "I never should have said the things I did to you that night after the dance. I know now that you were hurting too, and I never should have treated you as if you didn't care."

"I was hurting all right," he confirmed. There was a pause before he added, "Amy used to talk about you all the time, Erin. She really thought you were something special." Erin remembered the essay Amy had written for English class about sisters, and she smiled wistfully. Travis continued. "She was always telling me what a great dancer you were and how you were going to become famous."

"She had plans to be a famous actress too, and she thought we'd work together someday." Erin twisted the cord around her finger. "We probably never would have, you know. Even if she'd lived. But Amy always planned *big*."

"I was pretty mixed up when she was in the hospital. I was mad, and I didn't know who to be mad at." Travis's voice seemed to be coming through a tunnel. "Screwy, isn't it? I've had a lot of girlfriends, but the only girl I ever wanted died." Erin felt dampness on her cheeks and wiped it away furiously. "I loved Amy, Erin. I really did."

"I know," she said. "I loved her too."

"I kept some pictures of her just so I'll always remember what that feeling was like. I'll never forget her. You gotta believe that."

"I believe you." Her voice was scarcely a whisper. "And I'm just sorry I treated you so mean. I—I guess that's all I called to say, Travis."

"Look, I'll be wrapping up exams this week, then I'm coming home. Maybe we could get together and talk."

"I'd like that. It helps to talk about her." She thought of the items Amy had saved because they came from Travis. "There were some things in her stuff you might like to have. Pennants, a necklace—stuff like that."

"Sure," he said. "That would mean a lot to me.

And—uh—thanks for calling, Erin. It always bothered me that you were so angry at me. I feel better about it now."

"So do I," she said, and she meant it.

"Well, I gotta get back to the books."

"And I've got someplace I have to go."

"Good-bye," Travis said.

"Good-bye," she told him, and hung up the phone. She took a long, shuddering breath. Her head felt light, but it didn't hurt, and the tenseness along her shoulders evaporated with a few shrugs. She felt drained, but also at peace.

Still clutching the receiver, Erin rested her forehead on the wall. She closed her eyes. "Good-bye, Travis," she whispered. "Good-bye, Amy. Good-bye."

Chapter Twenty

Erin stood at the chain-link fence looking over the crowded track and infield. Banners flapped in the afternoon breeze. The biggest one read: Special Olympians—You're Winners! The infield was a jumble of athletes in gleaming wheelchairs and orthopedic braces, of bright T-shirts emblazoned with the five Olympic circles, of coaches and paramedics dressed in shorts and baseball hats.

Erin scarcely saw them. She was looking for David, knowing that even if he glanced over toward the fence, he would not recognize her. After all, he'd only seen her once in her full clown makeup.

All at once she saw him. He was making balloon animals for a group of kids swarming around him near a refreshment stand. She ambled toward him, her hands deep in the pockets of her oversize, baggy pants. She asked, "Need some help?"

"I sure do, here—" He stopped midsentence and stared at her. "Hey, I've seen you before." His brow crinkled beneath his whiteface, and his orange drawn-on mouth puckered. "Last year!" He snapped his fingers. "The Children's Home."

"Someplace else too."

"Erin?" His amazed, comical expression made her laugh out loud. "But—but—who? How . . . ? *You* were the girl who worked with me that day?"

"Yes."

"But you never said anything about it all this time."

"It's a long story."

"The girl who was supposed to appear—"

"Was Amy, my sister."

David shook his head as if to clear it. "Man, am I confused."

"I'll let you buy me dinner and explain everything after the Olympics are over today."

"But I thought you weren't coming."

"I changed my mind. And besides, some clown once told me that helping out and making people laugh makes a person feel good inside."

David came closer, ignoring the kids who began to scatter as the start of various events were announced over the PA system. "I thought you were brushing me off. After the play and all, you hardly spoke to me."

"I had a lot of things to figure out. Are we still friends?"

He smiled, and she felt as if the sun had just splashed over her. "I'll be your *best* friend." He took her hand and led her over to a grassy spot, away from the bustling activity. There he stood facing her, still holding her hand. "I got accepted to clown school for the summer."

"And I'm going to Wolftrap for sure. The scholarship's for three weeks."

"So are you all right now?"

"I will be," she said. "Our whole family's going to counseling now, and I also go to the grief support group for teens. Dr. Richardson's been urging my parents to start attending a Compassionate Friends meeting—that's a support group for parents who've lost kids."

David nodded. "I guess it helps to be with people who've been through the same things you have, huh?"

"It helps a lot."

"What about FSU in the fall?" David asked. "Will you be going there?"

Erin shook her head. "I'm going to start at the junior college, and if Dr. Richardson thinks I'm ready, I'll transfer to FSU at midterm. Otherwise, I'll transfer next fall."

"I know how much you were counting on going."

Erin shrugged. "I wasn't as ready to move away as I thought I was. Beth was excited when I told her. We're going to try to take a class together."

"I guess your parents are glad too."

"Relieved, I think. We're learning a lot about our feelings. What are you going to do in the fall?"

"I'm going to FSU to major in drama. My dad's not nuts about the idea, 'cause he really wanted me to go to law school, but I can just picture myself plea bargaining—if things got tense, I'd squirt the judge in the face with a plastic flower and get thrown out of court."

Erin giggled, and David studied her. "So when

you do get up to the campus, I'll already be there. Will you look me up?"

She sought his eyes through layers of grease-paint. "You can count on it," she said. In that moment she felt as if they were the only two people in the world, and that the sunshine and the blue sky had been created just for them.

She heard the sound of running feet and glanced away from David's eyes to see Jody run up with a friend.

"Guess who this is," David signed to his sister.

Erin awkwardly spelled out her own name, and Jody's face lit up with a grin, so similar to David's. She hugged Erin's waist.

"I think she's missed you," David said with a laugh. "She's running in a race soon and wants us to come and watch."

"Tell her I wouldn't miss it."

Jody stooped down and tugged up a handful of dandelions and shoved them toward Erin. Erin felt her breath catch and her eyes fill as she took the yellow bouquet.

"Are you crying?" David asked, incredulous.

"Tell Jody that dandelions are very special to me." Erin touched the soft yellow petals, remembering seeds floating away in the breeze at Amy's funeral. She held out her hand, carefully tucking her two middle fingers against her palm and extending her thumb, forefinger, and pinky. "I love you," she whispered.

Again Jody smiled, and the smile washed over Erin like a soothing balm. The child turned, tugged on her friend's hand, and together they darted across the field toward the track.

David said, "I don't get it. Jody gives you a bunch of raggy weeds, and you start bawling. Girls are weird."

Erin poked one of the flowers into his buttonhole. "Didn't you know that girls get to cry over dumb stuff for no real reason?" She reached up and placed her palm tenderly along his cheek. "And so do clowns."

ABOUT THE AUTHOR

LURLENE MCDANIEL has been a professional writer for more than twenty years and has written radio and television scripts, promotional and advertising copy, and a magazine column. She began writing inspirational novels about life-altering situations for children and young adults after one of her sons was diagnosed with juvenile diabetes. She lives in Chattanooga, Tennessee.

Lurlene McDaniel's popular Bantam Starfire books include: *Too Young to Die, Goodbye Doesn't Mean Forever, Somewhere Between Life and Death, Time to Let Go, Now I Lay Me Down to Sleep, When Happily Ever After Ends,* and the other *One Last Wish* novels *A Time to Die, Mourning Song, Mother Help Me Live, Sixteen and Dying, Someone Dies, Someone Lives,* and *Let Him Live.*